FINDING ULFRED

ALEXANDER BUTTERFIELD

First published by

Alexander Butterfield

First Edition

Alexander Butterfield asserts the moral right to be identified as the author of this work.

All rights reserved. No part of this publication may be reproduced, stored or transmitted in any form or by any means, electronic, mechanical, photocopying, recording, scanning, or otherwise without written permission from the publisher. It is illegal to copy this book, post it to a website, or distribute it by any other means without permission.

This novel is entirely a work of fiction. The names, characters and incidents portrayed in it are the work of the author's imagination. Any resemblance to actual persons, living or dead, events or localities is entirely coincidental

Copyright © 2020 by Alexander Butterfield

Dedicated to:

My Son and Daughter, respectively Charles and Lynn.

With grateful thanks to:

Gordon, Joanne and Charles.

For the many chats, useful thoughts and ideas. Sometimes wild and crazy over many Friday evenings supping a cold beer.

Thank you.

CONTENTS

Prologue..1

Chapter One – The Slaughtered Lamb. 2

Chapter Two – The Day It All Began. 7

Chapter Three – The Journey Begins. 21

Chapter Four – Ulfred's Road To Hell. 26

Chapter Five – Ulfred & Ozil. 28

Chapter Six – The Package. 30

Chapter Seven – The Search Begins. 37

Chapter Eight – Henry. 44

Chapter Nine – Morana. 47

Chapter Ten – Family Ties. 50

Chapter Eleven – The Wooden Box. 59

Chapter Twelve – Dinner For Two. 69

Chapter Thirteen - Henry's Story 73

Chapter Fourteen – The Note. 79

Chapter Fifteen – Delilah..89

Chapter Sixteen - All Tied Up...92

Chapter Seventeen – The Warehouse. 97

Chapter Eighteen – Closing In..101

Chapter Nineteen – More Pain!..109

Chapter Twenty – Morana's Cabin. 114

Chapter Twenty One – The Hunt For The Double H Gold Mine. 123

Chapter Twenty Two – Gaining Ground. 125

Chapter Twenty Three – The Hunter Homestead. 128

Chapter Twenty Four – Closing In. 131

Chapter Twenty Five – Battery. 134

Chapter Twenty Six – Head For The Hills. 137

Chapter Twenty Seven – Onwards & Upwards. 140

Chapter Twenty Eight – The Double H Mine. 144

Chapter Twenty Nine – Ulfred & The Double H Mine. 150

Chapter Thirty – Double Trouble. 153

Chapter Thirty One – Layla 156

Chapter Thirty Two – Trapped! 158

Chapter Thirty Three – Morana & Haaken. 163

Chapter Thirty Four – Morana Runs. 167

Chapter Thirty Five – Haaken & Ulfred. 170

Chapter Thirty Six – Homeward Bound. 173

Chapter Thirty Seven – Escape To Goregate. 177

Chapter Thirty Eight : Bear Necessities. 179

Chapter Thirty Nine – Morana's Cabin. 193

Chapter Forty – A Time To Die 198

Chapter Forty One – Morana And Henry 203

Chapter Forty Two – Farewell. 205

Chapter Forty Three – The Hunt Begins. 209

Chapter Forty Four – Lost. 211

Chapter Forty Five – Cabin In The Woods. 213

Chapter Forty Six – What Goes Around. 215

Chapter Forty Seven – The Reckoning – Part One 217

Chapter Forty Eight – The Reckoning – Part Two 220

Chapter Forty Nine – The Slaughtered Lamb. 225

Chapter Fifty – Three Months Later. 227

PROLOGUE.

Pain! Such Pain!

Throbbing relentlessly, pulsating outwards in never-ending ripples of agony from his left hand and upwards through his arm, to explode deep inside his dazed mind. *Why such pain?*

Brutal in its driven intensity to cruelly force him from his unconscious state, a tortured groan of discomfort escaped from his dry lips.

Ulfred Hunter began to come to as savage pins and needles stabbed relentlessly through his arms and legs on top of the excruciating aching from his hand, making him groan a little louder this time.

More agony from his left hand, tightly bound wrists and feet as he gagged on the stinking foul-tasting cloth stuffed into his mouth. He could feel and smell some kind of oily hood or wrapping about his head.

His mind screamed silently, as somewhat irrationally he

thought. *Holy shit, my circulation is being cut off.*

His body jerked suddenly with an involuntary cramping spasm, making him bump his head hard against something solid in front of him.

He opened his eyes, only to see nothing but darkness...

CHAPTER ONE

The Slaughtered Lamb.

The noisy bar, aptly named The Slaughtered Lamb in the mountain mining town of Goregate became unusually quiet when the door opened. An icy blast of winter's frosty breath swirled past his denim clad legs and fur-lined jacket. The man reached back to close the door, blotting out the dark night, whilst carefully scanning the bar for any possibility of trouble.

The tall broad shouldered stranger, obviously a man of the outdoors, crossed the floor to the bar with a fluid cat-like grace. Layla, the barkeep, found her eyes trapped in a fierce hypnotic gaze from his hazel eyes that blazed with an intensity that seemed to see everything and everyone at once. Her breath caught in her throat as he smiled at her, revealing slightly tobacco-stained teeth with the tiny flash of gold in a ruggedly handsome face framed neatly by his close-cropped beard. Taking in the rest of him, she noticed

a lethal looking tomahawk strapped to his waist along with the large backpack he carried with ease.

Despite his formidable appearance, Layla felt irresistibly drawn towards the natural animal magnetism radiating from him. It was a strange primordial power coupled with something much deeper. Instinctively Layla knew she could trust this man with her life.

The men at the bar naturally shuffled left and right to open a space for him at the counter. Layla reached for the whiskey, poured a shot, and then retrieved an ice-cold beer to accompany the spirit. To her, he looked like a man with a problem on his mind and a thirst to quench. Nodding to her, he reached for the drinks, downed the whiskey, and proceeded to finish the beer in one long thirsty gulp followed by an explosive burp.

"Pardon me, ma'am," said Haaken Hunter to Layla.

Wow... He thought to himself. *It's been a long time since I've seen such a beautiful woman.*

"Same again, if you wouldn't mind," his low gravelly voice rumbled.

The uneasy silence in the bar broke as the conversation picked up once again, fueled in part by the curiosity that entered everyone's mind about the strange visitor. Smiling, Layla casually tossed her long dark hair to one side and spoke in a low voice.

"What brings you to these inhospitable parts of what the local folks call the hell that spawned hell itself?"

For a split second, incredible anger blazed from his eyes. It was enough to make her take half a step back in fear, only to hear a soft eerie chuckle break from his lips. The sound raised goosebumps all over her body, giving her the feeling that someone had just passed over her grave. He fixed her with a steely look that vanished as quickly as it appeared, followed up with a wide smile. His gold-capped tooth glinted in the light.

"Would there be any comfortable lodgings close by?" he inquired in his gravelly voice.

She went on to tell him of the only seedy place in town.

"Turn left out the door, walk on up this street, cross over the next two streets. You won't miss the Hotel Hope"

He reached for the second round of drinks and quickly gulped them down. After paying for the drinks with another captivating smile, he nodded politely, thanked her, turned, and quickly left as silently as a wraith of early morning mist vanishes into the warm air of a rising sun. A sudden gust of chilled air blasted in as the bar door closed behind him to mark his exit.

Layla stared at the closed door and thought about the black snarling wolf's head on the signet ring on his left hand. *Who is he?* She thought.

Haaken Hunter climbed into his Ford Bronco and drove off slowly. Sure enough, two streets up from The Slaughtered Lamb he saw the words Hotel Hope, dimly lighting up the night on an old neon sign that buzzed loudly, casting a pale yellow halo of light on the sidewalk below. From what he could see in the darkness, the Hotel Hope had obviously succumbed to the stranglehold of desperate times a long while back.

The look of neglect showed like the worn wrinkles of despair on an aging hag's face. Pulling up and parking alongside the curb, he climbed out of his vehicle and hauled his large backpack off the seat. He locked up, crossed the sidewalk, and pushed through the stained and cracked revolving door. He quickly scanned the foyer, taking note of several large cockroaches skittering across the worn and torn linoleum covered floor. Hearing a low growl from the far left corner, his quick glance took in a battle-scarred and mangy looking black cat glaring at him from green eyes while tearing hungrily into a large, luckless, twitching rodent. He strode silently yet purposefully up to the dirt-encrusted reception counter. The old wooden surface lit by a flickering overhead fluorescent tube highlighted a myriad of time-worn scratches upon its surface. Taking pride of place on the counter was an ancient, ornately engraved brass desk bell. Before he rang it the sound of a chair being pushed back, legs scraping across a worn floor grated harshly in his ears. The old man, who had been sitting behind a battered and rickety desk, appeared to creak painfully into a semblance of attention while calling out in a hoarse voice with a slight tremor.

"Good Evening sir," he said "Welcome to Hotel Hope. My name is Henry. Will you be staying?"

"Yes, have you got a clean room with a decent bed?"

"Room 7 is clean Sir, fifteen bucks a night."

Not sure how long he needed to be in Goregate, Haaken Hunter handed over three twenty dollar notes. Accepting the money, Henry indicated the register.

"Please sign the register, sir," he said.

The old man handed him an ancient but well-sharpened quill along with an equally aged inkpot. At the same time, he slid a pair of large keys across the counter. The old-style keys were loosely bound together by a narrow length of stained leather strap with the number 7 branded onto it. Henry seemed to conjure up the keys from out of nowhere. Haaken stared in amazement at the ancient writing instruments for a second before picking up the quill, dipping it in the inkpot, and scrawling his name in the worn and torn register.

Once done, he scooped up the keys with his right hand and headed for his room, shaking his head with a wry smile on his face. Henry's watery old eyes followed the stranger with a hint of recognition until he vanished from sight up the creaky stairs. He reached for the register, quietly rotating it to view the stranger's name. Scrawled in large bold writing were the words, 'Haaken Hunter.'

"My my..." muttered Henry quietly "The pup comes a-callin'."

Entering Room 7, Haaken flicked on the light switch to reveal a gloomy, timeworn interior. The wallpaper was faded, and a threadbare carpet tried valiantly to showcase an ancient brass bed standing proudly against the far wall, with a stained porcelain washbasin in one corner. The single window covered by dark dusty maroon drapes that perhaps long ago had boasted a glossy velvety appearance. Quietly closing and locking the door, he dumped his backpack on the floor near the bed and lay down on the lumpy mattress. He stretched his body, trying to ease his aching back muscles from the many hours spent driving the long road to get there.

Settling back and easing his head onto the pillow, Haaken Hunter began to reflect upon the events leading up to the present moment.

CHAPTER TWO

The Day It All Began.

It all went back to that damned dark day two days before.

Was it only that long? Holy shit! Seems more like five years. Where did the time go?

Such a beautiful late summer day it was. The sun just breaking the horizon to greet the new day with warm fingers stretching out to scatter the early morning mist into oblivion. Its glow briefly banishing the signs of the cold winter that was already pushing the last of the summer from the mountains above. Standing on the porch, Haaken lit up a fine Cohiba Black Pequeños cigar and inhaled the ultra-smooth smoke, perfectly balanced and teeming with notes of cedar, sweet spice, and a splash of cafecíto. He quietly looked out at the forest, twin tendrils of smoke curled lazily from his nostrils.

The fresh woody scent of pine bark filled the air, a daily pleasure to Haaken casually enjoying the early morning chorus of birds singing in the new day. Grabbing up the bucket of chicken feed from the storage bin, with rifle casually held in the other hand, he stepped down from the front porch of the old family home.

A fine looking log cabin, still proudly standing in the forest clearing so many years after his father had first built it. Here and there, one could see signs of repairs to the cabin where after time the weather had taken its toll after his father, Harry Hunter, had left on that fateful day. It had been just days after his and his brother Ulfred's sixteenth birthday,

Harry had gone off on one of his periodic business trips and had never returned. The family had had no luck at the time from the authorities in their inquiries after reporting a missing person. It appeared as if he had simply vanished from the face of the earth. Haaken had worked hard, with very little help from his brother Ulfred over the following twenty-three years to keep things going while caring for their ailing mother, Molly. She had been completely heartbroken with worry and sadness, sitting each day on the porch for the next three years after her husband had disappeared. She had spent her time staring down the mountain track with a forlorn look tinged with deep regret. Finally, she had succumbed to a terrible bout of pneumonia. Her small grave still kept neat and tidy, was always surrounded with pretty bouquets of mountain flowers to watch over her final resting place. It was a resting place with a fine view across the valley from the gently sloping ground further up the mountain behind the cabin.

Their large log cabin fitted naturally into the open glade. A beautiful stream flowed by to one side, constantly running with crystal clear mountain water fed from a place much higher in the mountains above. An idyllic, peaceful glade surrounded by one hundred and seventy-seven acres of prime mixed mountain conifer forest. Just how their father had managed to purchase such a large parcel of timberland was never made clear. The only answer ever given was that he 'got lucky'.

Another time while on one of his periodic business trips, Haaken's father had returned with a medium-sized timber cutting saw and planer which sat proudly beneath the high roofed open-sided barn a short distance down from the cabin. Haaken and Ulfred had grown up working the mill with their father. Both had become proficient at operating the long chain saws used to fell the trees, and had learnt to drive the tractor-drawn logging trailers from a very young age. Haaken had taken to the heavy physical work like a duck to water, while his slimmer and somewhat weaker brother, Ulfred, had struggled to keep up. Ulfred could wield a chainsaw with great skill, but compared to the taller and more muscular Haaken, he was no match.

He preferred to avoid hard physical work and used any excuse to get away and spend time in town. Despite their differences, the two brothers were very close. Haaken spent his free time roaming the mountain forests, becoming adept at tracking and moving as silently as a wolf through the undergrowth. His innate sense of danger, natural-born gut feel for understanding wild animals and most humans would stand him in good stead on more than one occasion in his life. Haaken Hunter had matured into a true mountain man. Peaceful and kind to family and the few he considered friends, he was always ready to lend a helping hand. A big powerful man of moral fortitude, he was not a person to be taken lightly.

The cut timber planks and logs were collected and carted away by large trucks pulling long lumber trailers to the timber mills and manufacturing companies. Haaken's hard work helped bring in a fair income that kept the family homestead and land in good condition. They were always tending to new saplings planted for future timber and regularly clearing wide fire breaks in readiness for any unfortunate infernos. However, over the years, the economy had taken a terrible downturn and life had become difficult.

Thankfully their father, Harry, would go away periodically on his business trips and always managed to keep the family finances on a pretty good footing. Sadly, things had gone from good to being extremely difficult after their father had disappeared and their heartbroken mother had died. In her last days, Haaken had tried to get her to talk about her early life with his father, but she would never fully open up, highlighting instead the bright times and glossing over anything sensitive.

He instinctively knew deep down, that there was an unknown and complicated issue regarding his parent's relationship.

It had taken a while, but now with improved timber prices, Haaken had managed to get the operation back on an even financial keel. The learning curve of becoming a businessman and having to become astute with handling the costs of running the business against getting the right prices for the timber had been tough for him. His humble savings and any spare money would be put aside for his and Ulfred's eventual retirement. At least that was the plan. The thought of retirement always made him smile ruefully. *If I live that long,* he would think.

 Stepping down from the porch he began to go about his daily chores. Taking the bucket of feed, he headed over to the coop where the chickens were clucking and scratching away in the dirt.

They sprinted to the corner of their pen to vigorously scratch and peck at the sunflower seeds and corn he flicked generously over the low fence. Haaken stood quietly watching them scratch around and feed. *I've had a fair number of eggs from this lot and a few fat Sunday roasts.*

"C'mon you lot..." he said quietly "How about some more eggs!"

Haaken headed back to the cabin and placed the chicken feed bucket back in the storage bin. He paused to look around at the forest, listening to the natural sounds of peace and tranquillity that surrounded him. Yet something was bothering him. Since rising from a comfortable night's deep sleep to the dawn chorus, a strange sense of unease, coiling like a slimy serpent in the pit of his stomach had begun to grow. He could not pin the feeling to anything specific, and with a small frown, he scanned the surrounding trees for any unusual signs or sounds. Haaken quietly walked over to the pile of short logs that needed splitting. Placing his rifle within reach should he need it, he grabbed the long axe handle, and with a low quiet grunt, he pulled the blade from the flat-topped stump.

Placing the first short log upright on top of the stump and with powerful swings of the axe, he began to split the wood in two. These split logs were to be added to the pile stacked up under the lean-to near the cabin, for the large fireplace, the old wood stove, and the boiler.

A short while later, just as he was working up a good sweat from the work, the growl of a powerful engine in low gear slowly making its way up from the valley below began to intrude upon the peaceful solitude. Haaken's sense of unease grew. Visitors were rare up here.

Haaken sank the blade of the axe into the stump, turned to pick up his rifle, and silently slipped into the dappled shade of the trees to watch. A good twenty minutes later, a large dusty black Ford SUV with tinted windows came to a stop several yards behind his battered old Ford Bronco. Silence descended upon the peaceful morning for a few seconds before being broken by the sound of the vehicle's doors opening. Three men descended from the Ford, one of them a small, thin wiry man that reminded Haaken of a weasel. This all the more so by the Fedora hat, pulled low, keeping his face in shadow.

The other two occupants of the Ford were large men. They moved out to form a protective barrier to the front and back of the man wearing the Fedora. Haaken could now see he was carrying a blood-stained package in one hand. Eyeing them warily, Haaken observed that the two large men were obviously cheap thugs and as such were armed. They all stood still near their vehicle for a moment, obviously casing the place to see if they could spot anyone moving around. Apparently satisfied, they began to move quietly towards the cabin, pausing near the rear of his Bronco, still appearing tense and nervous as they took a look inside it. The tense moment was broken by the ominous sound of Haaken's rifle being cocked closely followed by the raucous cry of a crow taking flight at the sound of the rifle bolt chambering the round. The three strangers instantly froze in place.

"May I help you, gentlemen?" Haaken's gravelly voice growled.

Three heads swivelled like marionette dolls in the direction of the voice.

Fedora hat appeared to be beginning to sweat a little. In a high reedy voice, he called out.

"Are you the one they call Haaken?"

"Who wants to know?" replied Haaken, his voice now several feet to the right of where it first was.

Again their three heads swivelled simultaneously towards the sound of Haaken's voice. The two large men, one of them with unusually large protruding ears, were beginning to tense up. Fedora hat's reedy voice replied.

"I wish to speak with you on an urgent private matter which concerns a member of your family. We want to talk to you. It's very awkward standing out here talking to the trees with your gun apparently aimed at us, show yourself!"

The words carried an almost insulting cocksure arrogance that raised the hackles on Haaken's neck.

"I am quite comfortable talking to you from here," he said.

"Who are you?"

Once again Haaken's voice had moved.

"My name is Ozil Renwick, I am looking for Ulfred."

His eyes darted about trying to see and hear where Haaken was hiding in the shadows. There was only silence, Ozil continued to talk, although a little more nervously.

"I believe he is your brother. Ulfred has been doing some special work for me."

Still silence from the trees. Ozil looked about even more nervously before continuing.

"He has disappeared. Two days ago I found a small package nailed to my office door. After opening the package, I found what I believe to be Ulfred's signet ring and what I think is one of his fingers…"

Still, nothing but silence greeted Ozil's statement. Feeling emboldened by Haaken's continued silence and speaking more loudly, Ozil now demanded.

"We want your brother! Is he here?"

Haaken continued to hold his silence while thinking rapidly. *This must be pretty serious if these ugly fuckers have come this far to find my brother!*

Not hearing any reply, Ozil, now with a sneer on his face, tossed the package he had been carrying into the dark shaded area from where Haaken's voice had emanated. It landed within an arm's reach of where he crouched. He quietly retrieved the package and slowly opened the blood-encrusted paper to reveal a severed finger that may or may not have belonged to his brother. The finger was tethered to the signet ring their father had given to Ulfred on his 16th birthday. He knew it was Ulfred's ring. The black Titanium and Steel snarling Wolf's head emblem was unmistakable; Haaken himself was wearing the exact same ring on his left hand. Both of them had received the special rings from their father on their sixteenth birthdays. Haaken and Ulfred were fraternal twin brothers. Not long after that their father had disappeared forever on his business trip. He had never returned, leaving the family totally oblivious to whether he was alive or dead.

Gingerly holding the bloodless severed finger, Haaken slowly rotated it, bringing in to view a small tattoo of a bleeding heart with the tiny Gothic letters 'MH' inside the heart.

Almost dropping the finger, he stared in shock as the disbelief showed in his face. It really was Ulfred's finger!

Haaken's mind instantly recalled the day when Ulfred had proudly shown him the tiny tattoo of the heart with their Mother's initials inside it: 'MH' Molly Hunter. *No, No, No!!* His mind silently raged. Stepping from the shadows with his rifle aimed at the intruders,

Haaken was about ready to question them for more details, when upon seeing him emerge from the shadows, one of the large bodyguards, namely big ears, panicked and reached into his jacket to jerk out his small revolver bringing it to bear in Haaken's direction. He fired a single shot that struck the tree next to him. Haaken's rifle spat flame, the sound shocking in its loudness as the bullet tore a bloody jagged piece off the upper half of the man's large right ear. Immediately a spout of blood and bits of ear appeared to spray away from the side of his head. The shock of the bullet along with the passing shock wave knocked the large man completely off his feet.

"He is not here!" Haaken barked furiously, covering the remaining henchman and Ozil with the rifle.

Even with the threat of his rifle, Ozil and his remaining thug moved with surprising speed, hauling their shocked, now very pale companion onto his feet and beating a hasty retreat back to their vehicle. They still managed to fire several bullets in Haaken's direction from another pistol as he hurriedly backpedaled and dived for cover into the shadows of the pine trees. The tires of the large black Ford spun furiously as it backed up, slid around, and roared off down the mountain track. The Eden like peace of the cabin and the surrounding woodlands area seemed to have been shattered forever. Gathering up the body part attached to his brother's ring and the spent cartridge, he placed them into his coat pocket and silently strode back to the cabin with a tight, ferocious look upon his face. He collected a spade that was leaning against the porch rail and sprinted back the short distance to the Bronco. He tossed the spade into the back, opened the driver's door, and paused as he placed the rifle into a specially mounted scabbard along the inside panel of the vehicle. It was in this rage that he stopped while mentally reprimanding himself, *Haaken Hunter! What the fuck do you think you are going to achieve?*

His mind angrily answered back. *Catch them up, shoot the bastards, and bury them!* Slowly calming down, he spoke to himself.

"Think and prepare, brother. Think and prepare..." he said.

Stepping back with rifle in hand, he slammed the door closed and leaving the spade in the back of the Bronco, walked calmly back to the cabin. An hour or two later he sat by the warm fire and recalled the last time he had seen his brother. He could not forget the harsh words said at the time. Haaken thumped the solid coffee table hard with pent up sorrow and rage. Try as he could, Haaken was unable to even imagine how his brother had come to this horrible moment, this frightening event in his life. *Good God, Ulfred! What have you gotten yourself into? Who was that arrogant bastard? What was so important or desperate that you would stoop so low as to work for such scum?* The worry in his heart and soul made him cry out in frustration. He did not want to believe that the gruesome body part actually belonged to his brother, Ulfred. He bellowed to the rafters and the silent mountain beyond.

"Where in God's name are you, Ulfred?"

He reached for the full bottle of Jim Beam Kentucky Straight Bourbon Whiskey, whilst lighting up another Cohiba. With a crazed glint in his eyes, Haaken Hunter proceeded to drink until he passed out in a fitful, nightmare ridden slumber.

The dawn chorus slowly eased into his befuddled mind as he carefully opened his eyes. His head throbbed from a self-inflicted hangover from hell. Grunting with the effort, he staggered off to the shower and immersed himself in the ice-cold jets of water that sprayed unmercifully from the showerhead. After several minutes he stepped from the shower, thoroughly numb but wide awake, and vigorously towelled his body down to get the blood flowing. Haaken Hunter was feeling seriously hungry. Going through to the kitchen, he set about cooking up a large breakfast of venison, scrambled eggs, fried onions and coffee.

He settled down at the kitchen table with his breakfast and a large cup of hot black coffee poured from the percolator that sat permanently on the edge of the old woodstove. He ate quietly and finished several more cups of the steaming brew. Now with a clear mind, he began to think of how he would find his brother, alive or dead. His twin brother, always ready with a smile and laughter, yet so very different.

Ulfred Hunter was definitely a footloose, often misguided lad, sometimes cunning to the point of scaring Haaken a little. Ulfred had become increasingly sullen and ill-tempered after their mother's death. No longer ready with a smile and laugh, preferring to binge drink himself into oblivion and refusing to help out with any of the daily work around the cabin and out on the homestead. Haaken could not understand how quickly his brother took to consuming so much liquor, as easily as a duck takes to water.

Soon he was showing definite signs of an increasing reliance on the booze to make it through the day. Ulfred began to disappear for days, then several months at a time. Sometimes two years would go by before he turned up only to disappear again, never telling Haaken where he went or what he was up to. It was almost as if an invisible hand was constantly drawing him away to the dark side. Haaken had tried reasoning with Ulfred, hoping this madness would stop or eventually wear off. Recalling the last time Ulfred had returned after a long absence he had looked pale, bloodshot eyes glaring constantly, his hands shaking from too much alcohol, constantly drawing on cigarette after cigarette.

Haaken had tried to convince his brother to stay off the drink and spend as much time as he needed at the cabin to dry out and let his system clean up. Ulfred had laughed at him, saying he was fine.

"Don't worry! I know how to take care of myself. I'm no alcoholic! I can give up any time I want…" he had said.

Then eagerly but twitching a little as his cravings began to dominate, Ulfred attempted to convince Haaken that he was soon going to find something that would set him up for life.

At the time Haaken knew he was daydreaming and only thinking of his next drink to replicate the incredible buzz of an alcohol-infused fantasy world of unbelievable clarity of mind. A buzz which would all too quickly become a grey and addled soup of mindless days blurring into one continuous loop of timeless nothing. He had said as much to Ulfred who had responded angrily.

"Nobody in the family ever trusted or believed in me!" he had shouted as he stormed out and left.

Haaken's thoughts returned to the present. *I must find Ulfred. But first I need to track down those bastards and question them.* Pushing back from the kitchen table and quietly rising from his chair, Haaken stepped into the lounge and walked up to the heavy, ornately carved coffee table.

He slowly pushed it sideways off the thick, well used hand-woven Turkish carpet. Rolling up the carpet exposed a large trapdoor set seamlessly into the floor. He bent down to pull up the trapdoor by its recessed brass ring. Descending the concrete stairs, a flick of the light switch instantly revealed a well-ordered basement with a large workbench against the far wall. Stacked neatly along each of the other walls were a series of locked steel cabinets. He proceeded to unlock several of them, flinging open the doors to show a multitude of weapons, tools, and equipment from a past life.

A life he had committed himself to for five years, and enjoyed with professional pride. A chapter in time that was sealed with chains, a dark vault hidden in the depths of Haaken's mind securely locked away with a solid steel door of a period that held the uncertainty of life hanging by but a mere thread.

Of moments of pure adrenalin woven through with time spent with nothing to do but wait for the call to action. Uncertain if one would survive the day, be killed, or have to kill to stay alive. The life of a professional soldier with an elite band of brothers in arms had been exciting but extremely tough. It had given an individual a surprising understanding of the value of life and the power of friendship, trust, and commitment to each other in order to survive the chaos and sudden loss of close comrades. The pride instilled in every recruit stayed for life. Haaken had no wish to enter that world again, unconsciously rubbing his upper right shoulder where he had taken a round from a deadly ambush in a dark dusty place in Africa.

His time as a professional soldier was done and he had served with honour. A period of life-changing experiences he had walked away from, abandoning the trappings of the modern world to seek the quiet solitude and peace of his mountain home. A place to find a life where the living and natural way of the earth brought much joy and peace of mind. A misty mountain retreat, completely off-grid and surrounded by thick forest and vegetation untouched by humans for hundreds of years.

The tranquil sound of the mountain stream bubbling and rushing along with pure mountain water nearby was music to his ears. It was broken only by the occasional sound of his rifle firing, bluntly shattering the peace and echoing through the trees and off the mountains for a brief moment when he hunted deer for the larder. Otherwise, the serenity of the place calmly flowed through Haaken and every living thing. This was his Eden. *Damn! Damn! Damn!* Just when life itself seemed to be almost perfect.

CHAPTER THREE

The Journey Begins.

Winter was stretching out its cold icy fingers. The early morning mist was low, clinging to the ground and obscuring the road ahead as Haaken, clad in a long fur-lined waterproof coat, bounced about on the seat of the old Ford Bronco. The battered bodywork surprisingly did very little creaking and squeaking. The engine rumbled smoothly as the vehicle made its way along the rough track leading from the cabin down the mountain to the valley below. His pack, bulging and heavy, lay on the passenger seat beside him carrying what he felt was enough to get him through the journey ahead. Haaken Hunter looked out at the passing trees and mountains. *So quiet and serene up here. Why did they have to come and destroy the peace and tranquillity of my home?*

Reaching the narrow bitumen road a good hour later, the Bronco seemed to sigh with relief as he turned left onto the smooth road and proceeded to drive towards the tiny one-horse town aptly named Solitude. With a population of only sixty and a good two hours drive away, the town served this quiet corner of peaceful mountain countryside.

Driving into Solitude, he pulled into a parking space outside the small country store where one could purchase all the basics needed for living off-grid. Haaken descended from the Bronco and stretched to ease his legs, casting a wary look around to see if anything appeared out of the ordinary. All seemed to be as usual in the sleepy backwater town. Stepping onto the boardwalk porch of the store, he walked up to and pushed the door to enter. An old bell tinkled as the door closed behind him on its spring to alert the storekeeper to an arriving customer.

"Hey, Haaken, how goes it with you?" said a voice from the rear "Been a while since you were last down here."

Georgio, the very rotund store owner called from behind the old wooden counter at the back of the store, smiling broadly.

Haaken returned the smile, the gold cap from his eye tooth glinting in the sunlight streaming through the large front windows.

"Georgio, my old friend, how are you?"

"Surviving day by day, Haaken, what brings you down from the peace of the mountains?"

The smile quickly disappeared from Haaken's face.

"Any strange folks come in here looking for Ulfred?" he growled.

"Nope, but I did notice a black SUV pass through yesterday. Some time later it came roaring back through here at speed,"

Georgio spoke a little too quickly while looking at Haaken oddly.

"What seems to be the problem?" he asked.

"They came up to my place looking for Ulfred…" Haaken answered.

He pulled the bloody package from a large pocket in his coat and tossed it onto the shop counter.

"What the fuck?" shouted Georgio, jumping backward in fright.

His eyes bulged in shock as he stared at the severed finger which was now beginning to smell a little.

Visibly shaken, he looked back at Haaken.

"Did you do that?" his voice croaked out with a tremor "I don't want any trouble, Haaken. Is that why those folks shot through here so fast yesterday?"

"No my friend, I did not do that. Those bastards brought this horrible package with them and threw it at me. They claimed it's Ulfred's finger and demanded to see him."

Speaking very softly, Haaken went on.

"Now Georgio. What did they say to you?"

Still staring at the grisly mess on his countertop, Georgio whispered in a small, scared voice.

"They came in here saying they were old business acquaintances of yours and quietly demanded to know where you lived. Now you know I don't like trouble, Haaken and those fellas reeked of it! I told them the way to your place"

Haaken replied, his gravelly voice tense with anger.

"Definitely not business acquaintances or anyone I know."

Quietly studying Georgio with an unnerving and penetrating stare, Haaken could see the harmless store owner had nothing to hide.

"Okay, Georgio," he said "Kindly bring me a small zip lock bag and a pack of ice cubes"

Only too happy to get away from the macabre scene on his shop counter, he sped off to the back stockroom. Georgio quickly returned with the items.

"What's the damage?" asked Haaken.

"No charge, Haaken…" said Georgio nervously "Please take it and go. Consider it a gift."

"Georgio…" said Haaken with a smile "I need a favour. I will be away for a while. Would you mind going up to the cabin and checking on things for me? Especially, feed and water my chickens. Check the place is secure from any bears trying to get a last meal before winter sets in."

"No problem, Haaken," replied Georgio.

Picking up the finger, Haaken carefully inserted it into the zip lock bag, along with a few ice cubes.

He pushed the zip lock bag with the severed finger, deep into the large bag of ice. Watching every move with morbid fascination, Georgio began to gag and dry retch, forcing long drools of saliva to hang loosely from his mouth. With a curt nod, zip lock bag, and the bag of ice in one hand, Haaken spun about and strode silently from the store. Wiping the saliva from his chin with a shaking hand, Georgio called out.

"Wait!" he said "I've been thinking about the thin one with the hat, his name, something about it was uh, familiar…"

Haaken paused for a moment, turning his head to look back with one raised eyebrow.

"Yes! Now I remember. It was a few months back a couple of fellas came through here asking if anyone around here had heard of Ozil Renwick. I told them none of us here know the name and then they asked if I knew how far it was to Goregate. I told them if they took the road north out of town to the high mountains for about eight or so hours, they'd find it."

With a grunt and wave of his free hand, Haaken quietly left.

CHAPTER FOUR

Ulfred's Road To Hell.

On that terrible day of dissent between him and Haaken, Ulfred had angrily raced his truck down the old track. He braked to a sudden stop as he reached the main road. With the engine idling he stared ahead, then stamping heavily on the accelerator and spinning the steering to the left, he roared off. Ulfred felt incredible anger and frustration. *Why could nobody understand him?* His thoughts tumbled about in his mind. *I will show all of them, especially you Haaken!*

Reaching across to open the glove box, he retrieved a half-empty bottle of brandy, unscrewed the top while steering with his knees, and drank down the contents. He tossed the bottle out the window, glancing in the rearview mirror to watch it shatter on the road behind him.

"Yeehaw!" he hollered.

He sped on down the road, weaving the truck left and right before straightening up.

Now, three months later, Ulfred smiled to himself as he thought of the woman he had just seen. A pleasant feeling of fuzzy confidence in his addled mind from the contents of half a bottle of brandy reached out comforting fingers from the depths of his stomach. From the moment he first laid eyes on her, he had felt a connection. Almost overpowering it had been. She had been walking towards him as he was sauntering along the sidewalk on the way to deliver a package and have a meeting with Ozil Renwick. His eyes were instantly drawn to her auburn hair, instantly glinting with fiery highlights from the sun sneaking out from behind a cloud to suddenly brighten up his day. Ulfred Hunter had never seen such a gorgeous woman. He had felt his heart pounding in his chest. *My God, is this love at first sight?* They had passed each other on the street in the mining town of Goregate. At the time he was sure he could feel her eyes were on him, examining him carefully and in great detail. *I have to meet her!* He thought.

Several hours later Ulfred Hunter pulled up at The Hotel Hope in Goregate. He climbed from his truck and headed up to his room and bed. After much tossing and turning, he finally fell asleep, totally unaware of the road to Hell he had just begun to walk.

CHAPTER FIVE

Ulfred & Ozil.

Rising mid-morning the following day, Ulfred, still with the mysterious woman on his mind, felt the urge to rush off to Ozil Renwick's office and tell him all about this chance encounter. Despite his affinity for alcohol and his inability to keep any money in his pocket, Ulfred had a natural ability to charm females of all ages. His natural good looks helped him to maintain a steady stream of women at his beck and call. Plus, he truly believed Ozil Renwick was his good friend.

Ulfred had met Ozil one drunken night when he was desperate for another drink and stone broke. The barkeep, Layla, was threatening to have him thrown out when this thin wiry fellow had stepped in to save the day. With a friendly helping hand he had seated Ulfred comfortably at a table away from the bar. After paying the outstanding bar tab to the angry-looking Layla, he even brought a fresh round of drinks back to the table. Thanking Ozil profusely, Ulfred had greedily swept up his glass and swallowed the contents with a greedy but satisfied look on his face. He had promised to pay Ozil back in full when he found some paying work. Ozil had then leaned over from his side of the table and spoken.

"I am looking for someone to do some delivery work for me. Perhaps you are that person. The pay is very good."

Ulfred had accepted the job without a second thought as to who this kind benefactor might be. At the time he had been too busy swallowing another drink to notice the cunning and calculated look in Ozil Renwick's eyes.

From that moment onwards, Ulfred had been quite happy in his new job delivering packages. Sometimes the work entailed driving to other towns, even catching the train for long-distance deliveries. The money he was paid for these errands was very good. It allowed him to indulge freely in copious amounts of alcohol and entertain many of the women who frequented the bars in the seedy lower end of town. He never once had the urge to look, or enquire as to what it was he was ferrying from place to place. The money he was being paid was fuelling his every desire.

Ozil Renwick was always friendly and in Ulfred's mind, he appeared kind and generous even to the extent of renting a room for him at the old run-down Hotel Hope. Despite its grubby appearance and cockroach infestation, Ulfred found the place suited him and the lifestyle he indulged in.

Ulfred Hunter walked a little faster on his way to Ozil's office at the warehouse near the railway station. He was eager to tell his friend about the most beautiful woman he had ever seen. But Ulfred Hunter could not help himself. The physical need and desire to drink was strong and he automatically turned into the first bar along the way. *Just a couple of drinks, then I'll go.* That couple of drinks soon became several before Ulfred finally left the bar and wandered off to see Ozil.

CHAPTER SIX

The Package.

Ozil Renwick was sweating with fear and worry as he sat nervously in his dimly lit office. The pain from the most recent assault on his body by his sister, Morana, was still too fresh in his mind. *Where the fuck has Ulfred disappeared to?* He pondered with almost simian like eyes that darted about, never settling on anything for more than a few seconds. *Damn! She was so evil!* Glancing furtively into the darkness that surrounded him, half expecting his sadistic sociopathic sister to appear and inflict more terrible pain on his body.

He had limped into his office a minute or so after ten in the morning, just as the phone began to ring. He picked up the receiver and collapsed backward into his comfortable leather chair.

"What?" he said abruptly.

Hearing her sultry voice, Ozil sat bolt upright, eyes wide open, staring at the opposite wall.

Instantly he concentrated on her voice as she issued a set of clear and precise instructions.

"You will receive a small but very important package that I want to be delivered to me immediately," she said. "Failure to do so will be most unpleasant for you my dear. Make sure that new fellow, your most recent gullible underling, Ulfred Hunter is the one to bring it to me…"

The phone cut off immediately before he could respond. Ozil sat still as several fresh droplets of sweat ran down his forehead while he stared at the notes he had quickly scribbled down while his sister, Morana, had given her instructions.

Important package coming.

Deliver fast to Morana at the cabin on old mine site.

Only Ulfred to deliver the package.

Ozil Renwick liked his office tucked away, up on the mezzanine floor of the old abandoned warehouse near the railway station at the bottom end of town. Yes, he liked this stale dark place. His, very own quiet refuge away from her, yet not completely free of her. His sister Morana had been instrumental in finding the dusty old warehouse. It suited their needs as an out of the way place for pursuing their crooked business transactions. A vile business cooked up out of her demonic mind as she wove her web of deceit around most of the high powered business tycoons in the town and further afield.

Using her feminine wiles of incredible beauty and her luscious body to ensnare these men, Morana quietly but ruthlessly bled them of their fortunes, reaping their wealth like a silent thief in the dark of night. She watched their wives, fiancées, girlfriends, and children with sadistic sensual pleasure, as she connived to suck their very livelihoods out from under their noses without any of the fools realizing it. He watched her gloat daily in her secret world as she lined her pockets with their wealth. Ozil Renwick giggled nervously as he looked about the office. Unbidden thoughts lurked in the dark confusing maze of his timid mind. *Perhaps, one day I can make it all mine.* Always the phone would ring with her voice ready to give him instructions to send a package here or collect a package from there.

He knew full well there was cash in the packages but also knew from harsh experience, not to tamper with them. Ozil's one missing digit, his big toe, was an extreme, all too permanent reminder of her sick and sadistic ability to inflict pain on anyone who crossed her. No matter how small the error!

Half an hour later his office door opened abruptly, and in walked a heavily tattooed, swarthy complexioned man who placed a box-like package wrapped in a beautiful red silk cloth on the desk. The man did an about-turn and left immediately. Ozil Renwick stared at the package for several minutes while the large wall clock ticked the seconds away loudly. He had never seen a package like it. The longer he stared at the silk cloth, the more his curiosity grew, overriding his recent painful experience at her hands. His eager curiosity got the better of him. *Just a quick look…* he thought. Ozil's face became more weasel-like, as the need to know the contents of the package overcame his fear of her.

This time he would be extra careful, so she would never know he had looked. He reached slowly across the desk to touch the strange package. His stubby fingers lightly caressed the soft silk before gently bringing the package closer towards him. With an intent gaze, he committed to memory exactly how the silk was wrapped around the package, making sure there were no hidden threads that would alert her to any tampering.

What could be so important about this particular package? Why has she asked specifically for Ulfred to deliver it? With the utmost care, he very slowly removed the silk wrapping to reveal a highly polished and well crafted rectangular wooden box. A small frown of concentration furrowed his brow as he turned it over several times and listened. No sound of any loose objects issued forth from the box. He could not see or feel any obvious way to open it.

He then began to push and press the surfaces of the box to see if a hidden pressure point might release a secret compartment. But it was to no avail. Nothing clicked or slid open. Ozil Renwick's greedy little mind became frustrated as a further ten minutes passed and still he was unable to open the strange box. Grinding his teeth and stamping his feet in a minor temper tantrum, he slumped back into the comfortable leather chair. Suddenly his eyes lit up as a memory from many years before sprang to the fore of his mind.

Reaching quickly for the large magnifying glass on the desk, then peering intently through it he began to minutely examine the boxes' every surface and corner looking for one or more tiny holes. A grunt of satisfaction exploded quietly from his lips, as with a crafty look on his face, he spied a minute hole near one of the corners. The abrupt sound of a car horn from the road outside made him jump in alarm, reminding him that the office door was unlocked.

Springing up, he quickly locked the door. Returning to his desk he pulled open the top left drawer to remove a small rolled-up leather tool bag.

Unrolling this revealed a series of fine steel picks. He selected an extremely thin one and began to gently probe the tiny hole in the wooden box. A quiet click sounded with the abrupt release of a small drawer like compartment popping out from one end of the box. Pulling the small drawer a little further out, he saw nestled within was the neck of a black velvet drawstring bag surrounded by the darkness of the drawer. Sitting back and mopping his sweaty brow, Ozil smiled triumphantly. Slowly he reached for the velvet bag, placing his thumb and forefinger on the neck of the bag.

A sudden piercing pain shot up his arm, as a tiny black scorpion hidden in the darkness of the drawer pierced the

tip of his thumb with its deadly stinger. Instantly sweat sprang from his forehead whilst he pushed himself away from the desk, and slammed backward into his chair with a startled yell. He clutched his throbbing thumb with his other hand. Wide-eyed, he stared at the shiny scorpion, now sitting on the neck of the velvet bag with stinger still poised to strike again.

"What the fuck?" he yelled.

Tears of pain blurred his vision as the adrenalin forced tiny beads of perspiration to pop up on his forehead and run down the back of his neck. Carefully he got up out of his chair, afraid to upset the tiny black scorpion in case it charged across the desk to plunge that nasty sharp stinger into him again. Struggling to stand, he crashed over the side of his chair as a loud knocking at the door startled him. He looked up in terror from the floor expecting to hear her voice at the door. Scrambling frantically to get up off the floor, he let out a huge sigh of relief when he heard Ulfred's voice.

"Ozil! Are you there?" he said. "I heard a crash, are you okay?"

"Hang on!" said Ozil "I'll be right there…"

With a quiet sigh, Ozil used the long thin metal pick to push the drawer with the offending scorpion and velvet bag back into the wooden box. A soft click confirmed it was sealed once again. Hobbling slightly he walked around his desk, turned the key, and opened the door. Standing outside was Ulfred Hunter with a quizzical smile on his face.

"What happened?" he asked.

"Nothing!" Ozil replied with a scowl as he returned to his chair and sat down.

Strolling into the office, Ulfred casually studied the highly polished box on Ozil's desk. He wondered what could be inside it. Ozil began to carefully and meticulously wrap the box up with the beautiful red silk scarf. Still watching Ozil, Ulfred grabbed the wooden high back chair on his side of the desk, spun it around, and straddling the seat, sat down. A moment of silence descended upon the scene.

"That's a really smart-looking gift," said Ulfred "Who's the lucky girl?'

Ozil continued wrapping the box until he had completed the task.

"My sister..." he replied looking up from his work.

"She is a lucky woman!" exclaimed Ulfred, still admiring the package "By the way, speaking of women, I've just seen the love of my life."

"Really?" replied Ozil, raising his eyebrows and with a mocking tone.

"Absolutely," said Ulfred "The most stunningly beautiful auburn-haired woman in the world! I have got to meet her!"

Ulfred was clearly excited, his eyes wide, smiling at the memory. So enthralled was Ulfred by his feelings that he failed to see Ozil's face suddenly turn pale as he studied Ulfred with narrowed eyes.

"I'm sure you will," Ozil said, smiling back at Ulfred.

Ozil walked over to a cabinet to retrieve a plain cardboard box. He returned to his desk and proceeded to carefully bind the package in bubble wrap before placing it inside the cardboard box. Once he had finished sealing the box, he sat back and pushed it across to Ulfred who eyed it suspiciously.

"Ulfred…" he said, "Do you consider me to be a good friend?"

"Of course…" came the reply "Absolutely, Ozil."

Ozil fixed Ulfred with a slimy smile and held eye contact.

"I want you to take very special care of this package for me and deliver it, untouched, to my sister. It is vitally important you get it to her in one piece. Do not deviate for any reason. No drinking or pretty women. Do you understand?"

"I will make sure it gets to your sister" he replied nodding eagerly "Safely and in one piece."

"Good!" said Ozil.

"What's her name?" asked Ulfred.

"Morana…" replied Ozil with a tight smile.

CHAPTER SEVEN

The Search Begins.

As he left the store and climbed back into his Ford Bronco, Haaken thought about what Georgio had just said. He began to wonder what the connection was between Ulfred, Ozil, and the town of Goregate. In the rearview mirror of the old Bronco, the sleepy one-horse town of Solitude disappeared from sight as he drove around a bend half a mile out of town on the road to Goregate. He wondered what he would find when he reached his destination.

Reaching into his top right pocket, he fished out a half-smoked cigar. He lit it, enjoying the aroma. Haaken settled down for the long ride. It was a good thing he had a brand new V8 engine fitted to the old Bronco along with an upgraded suspension and braking system. As the miles passed, the terrible image of his brother Ulfred lying dead or injured in some dark place played like a movie clip on a loop in his mind. He struggled to imagine what kind of trouble or unfortunate circumstances his brother had gotten himself into that had resulted in him losing one of his fingers. *Who was he involved with? How long would it take to find him?*

After a couple of hours driving and needing to stretch his legs, he pulled over at the first petrol station with a Diner for a pit stop. He was getting tired of thinking and had decided a couple of burgers and some fries would help. In fact, the thought of the burgers was making his mouth water. Getting back on the road, with topped up stomach and both the regular fuel tank and his specially fitted long-range tank full, he drove on with a renewed sense of purpose and attempted to force the doubts from his mind.

It was dark, windy, and freezing cold when he finally arrived in the town of Goregate. His headlights lit the main street as he drove slowly along until up ahead of him he saw a bar with a sign swinging back and forth in the cold wind. The eerie words 'The Slaughtered Lamb' were painted on both sides. Stopping outside, he climbed stiffly from the Bronco, stretched himself, and grabbed his backpack off the seat. After quickly locking the vehicle he strode swiftly up to the bar door and entered. He had no idea that the woman he was about to meet would become an important part of his life.

Much later, after booking into his room at The Hotel Hope, Haaken had fallen into a deep sleep while reflecting upon the events leading up to that moment.

The following morning, the noise of vehicles moving on the street outside wrenched him from his deep slumber. He sat up quickly looking about at the strange surroundings, eyes scanning the room. *Easy fella. You booked in here last night.* Looking about the room, he figured it must be mid-morning. *I must have been completely exhausted. I don't usually sleep this late.* Swinging his legs from the bed, he eased his back as he stretched. He stripped off his shirt and t-shirt and opened the squeaky faucet on the chipped basin to get some water going. He plunged his head into the ice-cold water and brought it up quickly with a gasp, then grabbed the room towel and dried off. After dressing he sat down for a while and began to organize his thinking and ideas into a semblance of a plan. *Obviously, the barkeep would be a good place to start. She must know a lot about what happens in this town, and besides, she was easy on the eyes. What a good way to start the day.* He slipped a slim seven-inch double-edged blade with a smooth elk bone handle down the inside of his left boot, then slid his handy Tomahawk neatly through the special custom leather made loop on his belt. Finally, he tucked in his t-shirt and pulled his shirt down over his belt, before pulling on his warm overcoat.

Giving the room a quick check, he picked up his backpack and locked the room on his way out. He descended the old stairs quickly and passed through the lobby noting the mangy old cat sleeping off his rodent dinner on the wooden bench against the far wall. The old man, Henry, from the previous night was snoring quietly in his chair behind the reception counter. As Haaken pushed through the rotating door to the outside, old Henry opened one eye to observe him leaving. He smiled to himself and closed his eye once again.

Haaken pulled his coat close about him as the frigid air outside the hotel pushed the wind chill factor down to almost freezing. He cast a cursory glance at his Bronco to make sure all the wheels were still there and no evidence of a break-in could be seen. Haaken shouldered his pack, turned right, and with head slightly bowed, he headed along the sidewalk towards The Slaughtered Lamb. Once there, he opened the bar door and quickly entered, closing out the cold winter air behind him as he strode across to the bar counter. Dropping his pack on the floor next to him and opening his coat in the warm air from the large fireplace at the far side of the bar, he settled down on a stool.

Looking up, he saw Layla heading towards him along the other side of the bar with a smile.

"Hi…" he said "Sorry about my bad manners last night, I'm Haaken. What's your name? I can't keep calling you barkeep"

"Layla" she replied with a laugh "What can I get you?"

Haaken chuckled quietly. A deep rich sound as he glanced around the bar, which at this early hour was practically deserted.

"Please could I have a cold Coca-Cola and something to eat if possible?"

"One cold coke coming up and I'll get cookie to rustle up some ham and eggs for you."

She passed him the drink and went off to the hatch behind the bar to order the food. Quietly returning with a cup of hot coffee, she came to a stop opposite where Haaken sat.

"So…" she said, "What brings you here?"

He looked at her while quietly admiring her beauty.

"I am looking for my brother" he replied, "and a few folks he is involved with."

Layla took another sip from her coffee.

"What's your brother's name?" she asked.

"Ulfred. Ulfred Hunter. Have you met him? Does he frequent this place? He likes to drink."

Haaken noticed a slight tremor in her hand as she placed the coffee cup on the counter.

"Ulfred?" she said nervously "Yes, I do know your brother, and yes, he is a heavy drinker…"

"I hope he doesn't owe you any money?" Haaken asked, watching her closely.

"No…" she replied with a touch of venom in her voice. "Not anymore. Not since that horrible Ozil paid his debt. Now your brother works for him."

A shout from the hatch got her attention.

"Excuse me a second, looks like your ham and eggs are ready," she said.

Layla returned carrying a large plate of ham and eggs which she placed on the bar top in front of him. Haaken promptly and gratefully attacked the fine-looking meal with the enthusiasm of someone with a serious hunger to satisfy. He looked up, munching with his mouth full, and nodded his appreciation with another smile. He quickly finished the meal and ordered a beer. When Layla returned with the drink he thanked her for the meal and asked her about the history of the bar. Layla soon found herself explaining to this man, this stranger, Haaken Hunter, whom she hardly knew, but instinctively felt a natural bond for, that her parents had run the place until they were too old to continue.

She had been the owner of the place for a good five years now. Haaken nodded his head as she talked. He liked the way her voice sounded.

"I don't want to upset you Layla," he said "But I did notice you don't like talking about this Ozil fellow. Would you mind telling me as much as you can about him?"

Layla smiled.

"That's okay…" she said.

At that moment a couple of regular patrons walked in and Layla went off to serve them.

Where are you Ulfred? Haaken thought quietly while sipping his beer. Layla returned after serving her regulars some drinks.

"Where were we?" she said "Oh yes! You were asking about Ozil. That would take a while to tell…"

"What about telling me over dinner tonight?" asked Haaken "Is there anywhere private we could eat and talk?"

"You're certainly not shy, are you?" Layla teased him lightly.

Then, with a serious look on her face, she spoke.

"There are some fancy places to eat, but not very private. Do you mind if I suggest you come back here just after 10.00 pm tonight? That's when I close the bar and lock up. We can talk in the kitchen at the back. I will organize some dinner and of course, there will be no prying eyes."

"Yeah, sure," said Haaken with a chuckle "That sounds like a great idea. I would like that very much, thank you."

Haaken ordered another beer which she delivered immediately.

"I think I'll go for a quiet walk around town," he said, "I'll catch up with you later tonight for some dinner."

With a happy smile, Layla moved on down the bar to serve more patrons. The bar was slowly filling up for the afternoon.

Haaken quietly sipped his drink while studying the folks coming into the bar.

When the beer was finished, he rose from his stool, shouldered his pack, and raised a hand politely to Layla to get her attention. She nodded at him as he headed out into the frozen afternoon.

Once outside, Haaken pulled up the fur-lined hood of his long coat and took a long slow walk around the town to better understand the lay of the place. Eventually, he circled back to the hotel as it was getting dark. After a quick check on his vehicle, he headed upstairs to his room noting Henry was not in his usual chair. The cat was still asleep on the wooden bench by the far wall.

Stretching out on the bed, with the wall radiator turned up to full, Haaken tried to formulate a plan. But with so little information to go on, it was proving to be extremely frustrating. On the positive side, he was definitely organized for dinner with Layla later, and hopefully, she would be able to give him some information on Ozil Renwick and maybe an insight into what Ulfred had been up to these last few years.

With his eyelids getting heavy and closing, Haaken Hunter dozed off.

CHAPTER EIGHT

Henry.

The quiet scratching sound coming from his bedroom door instantly aroused Haaken from his slumber. Slipping silently from the bed and drawing the seven-inch blade from his boot, he padded over to the wall next to the door. Placing the blade in his mouth and gripping it with his teeth, he carefully turned the key in the lock and swung the door inwards. There was a sudden gasp as a small person fell headlong into the room clutching what looked like a note in one hand and master key in the other. Haaken stared down in surprise to see the old man, Henry, from the reception, lying face down on the floor. Bending down, Haaken easily rolled him over and lightly pressed the point of the sharp blade just under Henry's right eye. Henry tried to clear his throat while staring up at Haaken along the sharp blade. His eyes were wide with fright and his hands desperately waved wildly about to show he was no threat.

"I mean you no harm," he croaked "I didn't realize you had come back to your room. Please. I just wanted to give you these items and ask if you would meet with me tomorrow. I have something important to tell you…"

Haaken reached down to take the old man by the hand and hauled him to his feet.

"Fucking hell, Henry. I could have dispatched you from this life..." Haaken growled at him.

"I'm sorry" came the reply "I knew your father and I wasn't sure if you had come to settle a few scores here in Goregate."

With a puzzled look on his face, Haaken spoke.

"What the hell are you blabbering on about, Henry?"

"Please can I sit down?" Henry begged, still shaking from his surprise tumble and gasping for air.

"Sure," said Haaken guiding him over to the bed "Sit here."

Henry sat down gratefully and looked up at Haaken.

"You look remarkably like your father, you know?"

"How and where do know my father from?"

"Your father and I go a long way back to when we were working on the old gold mine just out of town."

"What?" said Haaken "I never knew he had ever worked on any gold mine."

"Yes, he did," said Henry quietly.

"We worked together, and I got to know him well."

"How long ago was this, Henry?" asked Haaken.

Clutching an old black and white photo with the note, Henry nervously passed them to Haaken.

Haaken placed the note on the bed while he studied the photograph.

"There are three people here," he said "You and my father I recognize, but not this woman?"

"The young woman you see in the picture is my sister Delilah." said the old man.

Haaken frowned, sensing Henry had more to say. At that moment the distant insistent ringing of someone impatiently pounding the front desk bell interrupted Henry's thought process. He eased himself off the bed and looked at Haaken.

"Could we continue this conversation over breakfast tomorrow morning in the hotel dining room?"

"Sure, Henry." said Haaken.

Rising to his feet, Haaken escorted the old man to the door and watched him shuffle off along the corridor back to the reception desk downstairs.

CHAPTER NINE

Morana.

Born with the face of an angel, Morana Renwick was five years old when she first became aware that she was different from the other girls and boys around her. This strange feeling of power gradually grew from year to year and once into her teens, she found an intense primal and sexual pleasure in the manipulation of others. The ever-present whispers in her highly intelligent mind worked in unison with an uncanny ability to totally recall everything and anything she saw or heard. This rare eidetic memory

was both a blessing and a curse. Initially, she had been totally absorbed in honing her evil skills by practicing the act of inflicting as much pain and terror as possible on her younger brother, Ozil. Eventually, she had gained total and absolute control over every aspect of his life.

Morana was so cunning with perfecting her evil dark skills on poor Ozil that everyone believed he was simply a hapless and accident-prone idiot. He had tried to tell his Mother - and anyone else who would listen to his tales of woe, that it was she, his sister, who was to blame for all the terrible things that befell him. But it was to no avail.

The immense power she felt, hidden from all by a shy, demure smile coupled with her exquisite beauty ensured no one would ever believe she was capable of such acts.

Seeing all others as fools, her twisted mind revelled in the seductive power of total dominance of these lesser beings. This power, coupled with complete control, made her

physically shiver with a deep and lustful desire.

With absolute certainty and conviction, she repeated her mantra daily. *I am the greatest. I can have total control of anyone I choose.*

By the time she was eighteen, Morana Renwick had become proficient in using her body and extreme cunning to extort money from most of the wealthy businessmen and influential players in Goregate. All of these men willingly paid what she demanded because of one thing. They were afraid of her. They were afraid to lose their power and lifestyles and terrified of what she would do to their families.

Morana Renwick was exceptionally gifted at gleaning information about their businesses and families, right down to their most intimate details and secrets.

This knowledge had proved to be extremely lucrative. Her mind was a seething, twisted entanglement of greed, lust, and overwhelming drive for absolute power. An endless mantra constantly pulsated through her brain. *I will have it all. I will take it all. I will. I will. I will!*

Morana had, after only a few years, secured enough money to finance the opening of her first upmarket ladies' apparel store. This stocked only the best and latest in fashionable ladies wear, lingerie, and must-have accessories. The shop allowed her to meet, mingle and socialize with the upper crust of the town. She had bold plans to expand and grow her business into an empire. With her evil cunning mind and her claws deeply embedded in their financial pots, she used every opportunity to secure power over the weak-minded men in her little black book, and become an integral part of their family's daily lives. Morana Renwick glowed with satisfaction every time a sale was made.

Not many people in Goregate knew who had purchased the old abandoned warehouse down by the train station.

Morana had purchased it using a shelf company.

The warehouse, with its dingy old office on the mezzanine floor, was the perfect place for her brother to operate the secret collection and distribution of her finances.

One fine summer's day, a few years later, Morana Renwick discovered how truly evil she actually could be.

CHAPTER TEN

Family Ties.

Morana Renwick had blossomed into a stunningly beautiful woman. A tall, green-eyed, statuesque brunette, she had full sensuous lips that enhanced an angelic face with almost translucent alabaster like skin. Her mother, Delilah, also once a pretty woman, was now haggard and drawn from massive alcohol abuse and chain-smoking. For as long as she could remember, Morana had never known who her and Ozil's father was. When asked, Delilah had always maintained he had left when Ozil was born. She would then halt any more conversation on the subject by retreating into one of her drinking binges. Ozil was thirteen months younger than Morana.

For most of her early years, Morana had constantly cleaned up the clutter of empty bottles and stale, stinking ashtrays left scattered about the house daily, by her mother. The old house was painted with a shocking lime green paint on all the outside walls with black pitch tiles covering the roof. Morana hated the place, it was the only house of its colour on the street. She was becoming tired of cleaning up and looking after her mother, even though she now had Ozil doing all the dirty work. Delilah had slowly succumbed to severe cirrhosis of the liver along with a constant hacking cough.

She would spend her days spitting phlegm into a tissue torn from a toilet roll and then stuff the horrible wet mess into the cardboard inner tube of the roll with a violently shaking hand. A habit that Morana found absolutely disgusting as she could hear the emphysema bubbling up from her mother's heavily tarred lungs as it did its utmost to slowly asphyxiate her. Delilah had by this time in her life, begun to forget things, sometimes rambling on for hours about things past and quite possibly things imagined. Morana was convinced that, along with her mother's many ailments, dementia was setting in. *Maybe she will die and I'll be rid of the stinking old hag!* She thought callously.

The event that changed everything happened mid-morning one day as Morana was doing a little cleaning in her mother's lounge while Ozil was clearing the coal and wood ash in the grate left over from the previous night's fire. Delilah was still in a drunken slumber, rambling as usual, when quite clearly Morana heard her arguing and pleading with someone not to take her son away from her. Her mother then began to weep hysterically in her sleep as she begged this person not to separate her twins.

"How can you be so cruel to split up Morana and Ulfred?" she moaned.

Then abruptly, with a snort and a snuffle Delilah quietly slept on. Shocked into complete stillness, Morana slowly turned to look at her mother, her mind racing. *What!?* She thought. *A Twin Brother!?* The thought exploded in her mind. *Ulfred? Ulfred, that's the name of the drunkard that works for Ozil. I wonder?* Her evil mind schemed, demanding in its forcefulness. *I must know! Mother will tell me!*

During the course of the next two days, Morana cherished the whispers in her mind, twisting hither and thither, so cunning, yet diabolically clever in their dark evil ways as she sat each day staring at her haggard mother. Such a wicked mind, she felt sensuous shudders of pleasure as the plot began to grow. She could have just asked outright, but knew she would not be told what she wanted to hear, just more lies and nobody was as good at knowing a lie, or telling a lie, better than she was. Morana wanted the truth from her mother, and no matter what it took, she would get it.

Slowly savouring each day from morning till she slept, the whispers grew and blossomed into a plan. A devious plot that most normal folks would wake up sweating and terrified from should such thoughts or dreams descend like a dark storm upon their minds.

Early on the third morning, Morana rose with an angelic smile radiating from her beautiful face as she went through to the kitchen to brew up some coffee for her mother. When it was ready she poured a large cup of the sweetened black brew and walking quietly into the lounge of her mother's simple home, placed it on the coffee table to cool. After clearing away several empty vodka bottles, she sat down on the edge of their coffee table and stared at her sleeping mother with a serene expression on her face.

From the front pocket of the pink apron around her narrow waist, Morana produced a small vial of Psilocybin powder and poured it into the coffee while gently stirring the cup.

Cocking her head to one side, she leaned forward and lightly began to slap her mother's cheek. Stirring from her

drunken slumber, Delilah began to twitch her face as the annoying slapping continued. With an effort, she opened her eyes, still bloodshot from the previous night's bingeing.

"Mother! Mother!" called Morana "Wake up. Wake up. I have some lovely fresh coffee for you."

Still groggy with eyes blinking rapidly against the bright morning light, Delilah managed to raise her head to look at her daughter. Morana gently reached around to the back of Delilah's head to support it while she brought the coffee cup up to her mother's lips.

"Drink the coffee, mother.." she said, "You really need it."

Delilah began to slurp noisily from the proffered cup, almost choking at the speed it was poured down her throat. Morana crooned softly to her.

"Drink mother, it will help you."

Finally, the last drop of coffee went down with a gasp from Delilah as Morana casually dropped her mother's head back onto the pillow. Delilah closed her eyes and drifted off to sleep.

Quietly putting the empty cup back on the table, Morana turned to study her mother's face with an intense look of excitement as she waited for the Psilocybin to kick in. She knew the effect of the mushroom concoction would begin to work its wicked magic on Delilah's mind in five to twenty minutes.

While waiting for the moment of truth to happen, she remembered something she had read about playing mood music. Going to her music centre, she stood for a while thinking, then selected some quiet music with gentle overtures of peace, and made sure the track was on repeat.

With the soothing sounds of the soft music now quietly playing in the background, Morana felt like she had the perfect setting to learn the truth from her mother. She perched on the coffee table with an angelic smile underscoring the expectant look in her eyes. After about fifteen minutes, Delilah began to stir and mumble.

"Mother dear," Morana called gently.

Delilah opened her eyes, looking directly at Morana, who could see that her pupils were quite dilated already. Her mother looked into her face with a serene smile of euphoria and complete trust. Putting on her sweetest smile, Morana purred soothingly.

"Mommy, what happened to Ulfred?"

Instantly a measure of pain showed in Delilah's eyes, then she smiled again, obviously seeing Ulfred in her memories.

Quietly, Morana began to brush her mother's hair; she knew it always calmed her.

"Mommy.." Morana called gently.

Delilah's eyes, now diffused with a happy, contented look, once again looked up at Morana.

"Mommy, please tell me about Ulfred."

Delilah began to reply.

"Yes Morana.." she whispered, "It is time, I need you to know about Ulfred..."

Suddenly she drifted off to sleep again. Struggling to contain herself, Morana had to get up and walk away before she grabbed her mother by the neck and ruined the moment.

Unfortunately for him, Ozil was just finishing cleaning the fireplace grate before going off to the warehouse office. He was still bent over and had just started to straighten up from the grate. Morana needed no further encouragement. She cruelly lashed out with a very expensive pointed shoe and drove it fiercely between his buttocks. Ozil shrieked in pain as he was launched off his feet and crashed heavily onto the wrought iron fire grate. He clutched his bruised ribs and his now extremely painful rectum. Stepping forward with an evil menacing hiss, Morana stood heavily on Ozil's outstretched ankle and bent down to his contorted face.

"Make another sound you horrible little waste of a man and I will snap your ankle so badly you will drag it behind you for the rest of your life!" she hissed.

Ozil bit down on his bottom lip until a little blood eased from the corner of his mouth as he stared up into Morana's glowing green eyes. He nodded his head in abject terror.

With a toss of her beautiful auburn hair, Morana turned back to her mother as Ozil crawled painfully away. Once he felt he was a safe enough distance from her, he got slowly to his feet and limped off to go to their warehouse office to receive and dispatch the daily manipulations of financial wealth from his sister's many hapless victims.

Morana returned to sit near her mother and commenced gently brushing her hair once again while crooning softly to her as a mother would to her baby. Delilah began to open her eyes.

"Mommy dearest" purred Morana sweetly, "Please tell me more about Ulfred"

Delilah looked deep into Morana's eyes and spoke.

"Yes, yes, yes. Ulfred my son, your twin brother..." she said quietly "He took him away from me, he stole my baby!"

Tears of pain and sorrow streamed down Delilah's face and then she drifted off to sleep once again. Morana ground her teeth in pure frustration and anger as she leaned forward. Her hands like twisted talons, with eyes bulging in sheer hatred as she stared down at Delilah. Quickly she took in a sharp breath and her eyes cleared as she stood up and calmly walked over to pour herself a cup of coffee. She stood with the steaming mug and gazed out of the window with a serene smile, while the peaceful, relaxing music played on in the background.

Carefully and neatly placing her empty cup back on the tray, Morana returned to sit by Delilah and began to gently brush her hair once again. Quietly she crooned to her until Delilah, once again, began to open her eyes with a smile as she gazed up into Morana's sweet smiling eyes.

"Mommy dearest," she purred "Who took Ulfred?"

Delilah's eyes widened briefly, her head craning forward a little as she spoke in a hoarse voice.

"Harry Hunter!" she croaked, "The Bastard! Took my Ulfred, you were only three months old!"

Suddenly she collapsed back onto the pillow and drifted off once again. Clenching her hands tightly, Morana looked up at the ceiling, exasperated but jubilant as she began to gloat. *Now I know who our father is!* Morana again looked down at her mother. She picked up the hairbrush and gently started brushing her hair while crooning softly to her as the peaceful music continued to play on in the background. *Harry Hunter?* her thoughts began to rapidly reassemble into a cunning maze of intricate manipulative evil. *I must find a picture of him! I will know everything about you, Harry Hunter!*

"You are going to pay, my dear father!" Morana whispered fiercely.

She gently pushed a stray wisp of hair from her mother's forehead as the horrible sound of the bubbling emphysema gurgled away in Delilah's chest.

Quietly placing the hairbrush on the table, Morana got up to pour herself another cup of coffee. She walked over to the antique roll top desk and sat down before it. Pulling a key from a long silver chain around her neck, she unlocked the desk and opened it. Reaching into one of the pigeon holes, she pulled out a small folded note and read the message on it with a frown on her face. *I don't like puzzles!* she thought to herself as she pocketed the note. Picking up the phone she dialed the office number, fully expecting Ozil to be there waiting for her daily commands. He answered a little abruptly on the second ring, then after realising it was her, she heard him squirm. Morana smiled sweetly to herself.

"Ozil.." she said "What's the surname of Ulfred. The one you told me you found in the bar with a drinking problem. The one you said would be perfect for doing our bidding and not ask any stupid questions?"

"Ulfred Hunter. Why?" he replied, the question popping out of his mouth before he realised his mistake.

"Never question me Ozil!" she hissed"You know that will only cause you more pain!"

"Sorry Morana!" he stammered nervously.

She went on to tell her brother to expect a small but extremely important package for her and that she specifically wanted Ulfred, his latest gullible underling, to bring it to her at her cabin out of town on the old abandoned gold mine site.

She took great pleasure in reminding Ozil, that failure to have it delivered would be most unpleasant, and rang off before he could reply. Morana returned to check on her mother, who was quietly wheezing away, still sound asleep. *At least she isn't dead yet.* She thought with cruel disdain. *I still need more answers.* Then after gathering up her warm fur-lined coat, Morana Renwick left her mother's house for the old mine out of town.

CHAPTER ELEVEN

The Wooden Box.

Ulfred's eyes followed Ozil as he stood up to get some cash from a large safe in the corner of his office, before flicking back to the sealed cardboard box in front of him. In his mind's eye, he saw only the exquisitely polished wooden box inside.

Curiosity began to gnaw with the patient persistence of a rat gnawing through wood. Ozil returned to his seat, looking at Ulfred as he pushed some cash across the table.

"Ok Ulfred, here's what I want you to do."

Taking up pen and paper, Ozil began to write down directions for Ulfred, on how to get to his sister at the mine site. Handing them to Ulfred, he spoke.

"Remember, straight to my sister, no deviating!"

Ulfred stood up, tucking the directions in his shirt pocket, and picked up the package.

"Don't worry Ozil, I've got this" he said and with a smile on his face, Ulfred left.

Once out of the warehouse, he walked briskly into town towards the hotel several blocks away.

Hunched up against the cold icy wind, Ulfred could still hear that persistent rat gnawing away at his subconscious. *What's in the box Ulfred?* Arriving at his parked truck outside the Hotel, Ulfred carefully placed the box on the seat next to him before starting up the motor to get some warm air blowing through the vents. *Damn it's freaking cold. Well then, I had better get this up to Ozil's sister and get back for some drinks at the bar tonight.*

Pulling out into the road, he drove out of town, heading up into the mountains. Thinking about Ozil's sister automatically brought to mind a vision of the stunning brunette he had seen on the sidewalk earlier. *Who was she?* He pondered this as he drove along, instinctively reaching for the glove box to take out a bottle of brandy. Pulling the stopper with his teeth and spitting it onto the seat next to the box, he took a long enjoyable swig, momentarily closing his eyes to savour the strong liquor. Then gripping the neck of the bottle and the steering wheel with the same hand he reached down for the stopper with his free hand, taking his eyes off the road as he did so. It was only a second or two, but that was all it took for his eyes to stray from the road ahead.

A large moose wandered into the road in front of the

oncoming truck. When Ulfred flicked his eyes back to the road all he could see was the huge animal blocking his vision. Instantly panicking, he dropped the half-empty bottle and jerked the steering wheel to the left, effectively running off the road and down the steep-sided ravine. Ulfred screamed out in terror, stamping down hard on the brake pedal, but this only made things worse.

The back end of the truck started to skid round, causing the vehicle to roll over several times as it clattered and bounced its way to the bottom of the ravine, finally coming to rest upside down in a small shallow rocky stream. Silence descended upon the scene of the accident. The large moose, still standing in the road, flicked its head and trotted away into the forest.

Ulfred slowly came to, as the powerful scent of neat brandy pervaded his senses. His shirt was soaked with it and he was feeling cold, really cold. Now also aware of the sound of running water, he opened his eyes, groaning in pain as he tried to figure out what he was looking at. A trickle of blood dripped onto the roof lining from a large bump on his forehead with a long open cut across it. Gradually it dawned on his battered senses that he was hanging upside down, trapped in his truck.

"Shit! Shit! Shit!" he said.

Realising he had better get out of the cab, he frantically struggled for what seemed an eternity to release the tight seat belt bearing his full weight. After what felt like a long time, he managed it, instantaneously dropping his body a few inches onto the roof liner, into a worse crumpled up position balancing painfully on his bent neck. Squirming with great difficulty, Ulfred managed to ease around on the bits of wood from the broken box. Trying to manoeuvre into a more comfortable position, Ulfred suddenly let out a loud scream of pain. In the chaotic tumble to the bottom of the ravine, one foot had somehow been broken or severely sprained.

Blinking the tears from his eyes, Ulfred slowly crawled out from under the vehicle through what used to be the windscreen, now thankful to be alive. Warily taking stock of his aching body, Ulfred realised he had a serious problem now. *How am I going to get back up to the road before I freeze to death down here? Nobody will see me?* He wondered as blood from his cut forehead ran down the side of his face.

"Oh Crap!" he shouted out "The fucking box. It's shattered! How the hell am I going to explain myself out of this one?"

What was so damned important about it anyway? Ozil looked like it was a matter of life or death to make sure it gets to his sister. Mustering all his strength and courage, Ulfred eased himself around facing the truck to look for the remnants of the box and whatever was inside. Perhaps he could rescue the items. Lying on his less injured side, he reached in through the open door with his left hand searching among the broken shards of glass and wood splinters scattered over the roof lining.

Flipping over a larger piece of wood, he saw the velvet bag and hastily reached for it. Instantly his hand froze with his eager fingers a mere hair's breadth from a tiny black scorpion clinging to the bag with tail raised defensively. Too late! It struck with a vengeance, plunging the stinger, not once but three times into the tip of one of his fingers. Jerking back his hand with a howl of pain, he hit his elbow hard on the door frame at the same time. Ulfred raised his now throbbing hand to eye level to examine his ring finger. Beads of sweat broke out along his forehead from the pain as he shook his head in disbelief at the three tiny red dots of blood on the end of his finger.

"Where the fuck did you come from?" he shouted while rubbing his elbow.

Ulfred Hunter began to wonder how poisonous the little creature might be. Focusing once more on the small velvet bag, he noticed the small scorpion had crawled away out of sight. Keeping a wary eye open, Ulfred reached forward and grabbed the bag. Easing himself to rest his back against the side of the truck and sweating from the effort, he examined the velvet bag a little more closely. It felt quite heavy with something hard inside that seemed, by the sound of it, to be surrounded by paper. *Here goes nothing.* He thought, tugging gently at the drawstring with fingers that still throbbed painfully. Remembering the nasty little scorpion, Ulfred carefully upended the bag and gently shook it. Out fell a large gold nugget, the biggest he had ever seen. For several seconds Ulfred forgot the freezing cold that was now causing him to shiver quite violently and stared at the gold nugget lying on the ground.

"Damn..." he exclaimed "Will you look at that!"

I wonder if there are any more of you, he thought wiggling a finger around inside the bag. *Nope. No more.*

Still shivering, he slowly and carefully tugged the folded paper lining from the bag and when it came free, he grinned triumphantly. Picking up the nugget, he dropped it into the bag and pulled the drawstring tight. He unfolded the paper to reveal a detailed miniature map of some old mine workings, the name of the mine, 'The Double H', and what appeared to be the coordinates of where it could be found. Committing the coordinates to memory with a sneaky smile, he suddenly thought. *Shit! I might forget them. Where can I mark the coordinates down?* Picking up a small shard of broken glass, he scratched them into the door frame below the door catch. *Hardly anyone ever looks there.* He thought smugly. *Okay! Now I see why this package is so important.* He thought as he buttoned the bag, now closed with the nugget and map, securely inside his top pocket.

Even though he was still somewhat dazed from the accident and his discovery, Ulfred had a strange feeling that there was something familiar about the mine coordinates. He began to painfully ease himself slowly up the side of the ravine to the road. Fortunately, the ravine was not very deep and after about thirty minutes of much groaning through clenched teeth and almost passing out several times, he managed to reach the roadside. Ulfred collapsed gratefully onto his back and lay staring up at the sky, still sweating profusely from the agonizing short climb. He noticed a light mist had begun to descend upon the road and surrounding trees.

The growl, when it came, was low and menacing. It raised the hackles on Ulfred's neck as he slowly turned his head to look down the length of his body. Twenty yards away a large black Rottweiler stared at him, lips curled up revealing frighteningly large canines that could rip nasty holes in a person. *You have got to be kidding me!* He thought. He kept his eyes on the dog now slowly moving menacingly towards him as it placed one foot in front of the other, emitting a low but terrible sounding growl. His neck began to hurt from the strain of peering down his body at what seemed to be the biggest hound from hell he had ever seen. He tried desperately to think of a way to deal with the situation. Then through his slightly blurred vision from straining to keep his eyes on the dog, Ulfred saw some other movement beyond the dog. *Don't tell me there are more?* he thought miserably. He blinked his eyes rapidly several times to clear them and stared in amazement, thinking he must be hallucinating.

Quite clearly he could see approaching out of the swirling mist a vision of beauty, a beautiful auburn-haired angel of mercy, her face almost translucent with the fairest alabaster skin. *It's her!* His mind shouted out in excited relief, as he heard her angrily tell the huge dog to lay down. Ulfred blissfully passed out as he vaguely heard her voice fade away.

Much later that evening, still a little dazed and groggy, Ulfred opened his eyes to find he was warmly covered in a soft blanket on a large couch with the sound of a large fire crackling away not far from where he lay. Feeling a little better and recalling the earlier events of the day, he checked his finger which still ached, and tried to move his damaged foot. With relief, he found that moving it slowly did not hurt so badly now. *Must have just sprained it.* He also found his head was lightly bandaged, covering the cut in his forehead. Looking around the well-furnished lounge of a large log cabin he wondered where she was. *This must be her place.*

At the same time, he caught the faint scent of Chanel No 5 in the air. Another thought suddenly sprang into his mind. *The gold nugget and the map! Where are they?* Quickly reaching up to his shirt pocket to check, he almost shouted out aloud. *Oh Shit! It's gone!* Not only was there no nugget, but there was also no shirt either. He realized he was quite naked under the blanket. *Come to think of it, I wonder how I got here?* With a startled and worried look on his face, Ulfred turned his head sharply, wincing in pain as the sound of her soft sultry voice called out gently behind him.

"Hello, Ulfred," she said.

Craning his neck hard to his right and backward, Ulfred could just see her sitting in a chair several feet behind him with that damned big dog by her side. It growled with a low threatening rumble as its top lip slowly curled up, showing those large white canines. *This is very weird.* He thought.

She spoke again.

"Ulfred, my name is Morana. I have been expecting you."

The thought exploded in his mind. *Shit! It's Ozil's sister.*

Then again. *Dear Lord, I have been lusting after his sister! The very woman he is so terrified of.* He heard her rise from the chair behind him, the soft rustle of her skirt whispering against her legs as she walked past the end of the couch to face him. She stood staring down at him intently, her legs slightly parted with one elegant hand reaching slowly out towards his face as the soft material of her skirt moulded itself with a light swirl to her perfectly shaped legs.

Ulfred felt his loins stirring at the sight of her, with full ruby red lips framed by her beautiful alabaster white skin and long lustrous auburn hair. Looking up into her face, he could not help himself.

"You are so gorgeous.." he said with a smile.

Ulfred felt an instant bond looking into her eyes, almost like he was looking into his own.

With one eyebrow arched, Morana smiled sweetly. Ulfred barely had time to avert his face as the hand behind her back swung out and up, then viciously down towards his face with a short riding crop. The crop bit into the side of his face with extreme force. Ulfred yelled out in pain, now cowering back from Morana.

"What the fuck?!" he shouted, instantaneously losing all the sexual desire he was feeling.

Reaching down, she grabbed his hair and wrenched his

head back with surprising strength. Ulfred, his eyes now wide with shock, stared at a completely transformed face, filled with malice mixed with an animal-like lust. Her top lip curled up revealing neat but small tightly clenched teeth as she brought her face closer. Her hot sweet-smelling breath washed over his sweating face while she panted rapidly.

"You broke my package, Ulfred!" she screamed.

Her face flushed with what looked to him like more lust. Morana's tongue rapidly licked her full lips and then she lashed him again, almost groaning with pleasure. Abruptly standing upright, she quickly turned away and strode from the room, returning in less than a minute with a glass of water and a small first aid kit.

Ulfred sat hunched up on the couch clutching the soft blanket to his chest while trying to keep any parts of his naked body from showing. He barely had any time to figure out what had just happened. He simply stared at her in shock.

"Oh you poor dear.." she said sweetly as she brought the glass to his lips, "Here, have some water"

Watching her in trepidation, Ulfred sipped a little from the glass. Morana took the glass away, placed it carefully on a side table, opened the first aid kit, then proceeded to gently clean and dress the cut which, a moment ago she had savagely inflicted on him with the riding crop. His eyes darted about, trying to see where it was while watching her at the same time. *I'm in hell!* his mind screamed. *Did I die? How can someone so beautiful be such a maniac and then so kind at the same time?*

Morana gently raised the glass to his lips again, this time Ulfred drank thirstily while wincing as she reached out to gently touch his wound. He began to feel drowsy, then, passed out into a deep slumber. Staring down at Ulfred with evil intensity, Morana almost lashed out again. Instead, she reached down and lightly ran her forefinger over his lips, smiled, then quietly got up and walked over to a large writing bureau. There, lying on the opened lid, was the velvet bag and gold nugget resting on the opened map, alongside another note. Morana picked up this note, which she had found pushed under the front door to her shop. Sitting down with a frown, she once again read the contents of the note that had been signed by her loving Uncle Henry.

CHAPTER TWELVE

Dinner For Two.

After seeing off old Henry, Haaken decided to go down to The Slaughtered Lamb a little earlier than planned for a couple of beers as it would not be long before Layla locked the place up for the night. Wondering what Henry might have to say the following day, he picked up his backpack, locked the room, and left.

He was soon seated comfortably at the bar with a cold beer in his hand, watching Layla chatting and serving drinks. Haaken began to suspect that there were many more strange and complicated undercurrents in this town that could quite possibly, be very bad for his health.

Okay. What do I know so far? Apart from Ulfred's finger and ring, there is no sign of him. Folks seem to know him and Ozil apparently had him doing some kind of errand or delivery work. Lovely Layla owns the bar. And Henry? I'm not too sure where Henry fits in… He apparently knew my father. They worked together on a gold mine not far from town. There is also Henry's sister, Delilah? Hopefully, Layla might just fill in a few of the blanks and give me enough intel to start piecing this puzzle together.

Wearily shaking his head, Haaken finished his beer and waved politely at Layla indicating he would like another.

Reaching into the top pocket of his shirt to withdraw a fresh Cohiba, he lit it and inhaled, enjoying the cigar. He slowly exhaled with satisfaction as his mind wrestled with how to proceed. The sudden harsh clang of a steel rod being rotated inside the hanging metal triangle above the centre of the bar brought him back to the present moment. This announced that the bar would be closing in a few minutes. He glanced up to see Layla putting the metal rod back under the bar. After finally getting the last of the evening crowd out of the bar, Layla locked up the doors.

"I hope you're hungry," she said as she returned, "Follow me..."

"Starving," Haaken replied, grinning happily.

Easing off the barstool, he retrieved his backpack from the floor and followed Layla, noticing as they went through to the large kitchen that she walked with a slight limp. There, laid out neatly on a large old wooden table with long bench seats on either side, was dinner. Dropping his backpack on the floor near the table, Haaken eased himself onto the long bench seat on one side, while Layla eased in on the other. Picking up one of the dinner plates, she dished up a healthy portion for Haaken. After passing him the plate, Layla helped herself to a goodly portion, then popped the caps off two beers, pushing one across the table to Haaken.

"Dig in before it gets cold," she said.

An amicable silence descended upon the room as they tucked into the dinner. Looking up from his plate with a satisfied burp and smile, Haaken spoke.

"Pardon me!" he said, "Thanks Layla, superb food."

She bobbed her head a little with a smile, accepting the compliment.

"Ok, what do you want to know?" she asked reaching for two more beers.

"What can you tell me about Ozil Renwick?" he said taking a sip.

Layla went on to tell him Ozil was the younger brother to Morana. She said they were probably two of the most corrupt and despicable people she had ever met.

"Tell me more..." urged Haaken with a smile as he looked directly into her eyes.

Layla's hand unconsciously reached up to push a strand of hair from her forehead as she looked into his eyes. *Oh, Lord.* She thought. *I think I'm falling for him. It's been years since I've felt like this for any man.*

Then almost immediately, she stood up to collect the empty plates. She turned away to the kitchen sink before Haaken could see the bloom of a deep blush rise up her neck to her face. Quickly rinsing off the plates and stacking them on the draining board she composed herself and returned to the table.

It was after midnight before Haaken and Layla finished talking. He now knew where Morona and Ozil operated their shady business from. According to Layla, it was an old abandoned warehouse near the train station. Fortunately, Ulfred had let slip the information to her during one of his drunken bouts; apparently an all too regular occurrence.

Layla also felt sure that Morana was somehow receiving a substantial amount of money from some very important townsfolk through blackmail or something similar. Again she had gleaned certain information from Ulfred's loose lips after much drinking.

Glancing at the time, Haaken rose and spoke.

"Layla, it's later than I thought. I'm sorry for keeping you up. I would like to continue our conversation later tomorrow if that's okay with you?"

"Don't apologise Haaken," she said smiling with a light rosy blush highlighting her cheekbones. "I've enjoyed talking to you. It's okay to come by later tomorrow. I'd like that..."

"Thanks for a fine meal," said Haaken as their eyes met "I will see you tomorrow."

Haaken almost kissed her right then but smiled a little nervously instead. He picked up his backpack and turned to leave. Layla accompanied him to the door feeling sure he *was* about to kiss her.

"Good night, Haaken," she said as she let him out of the doors.

Pulling the fur-lined hood up over his head, Haaken smiled happily at her, waved, and left for the Hotel Hope in the bitterly cold darkness.

CHAPTER THIRTEEN

Henry's Story

Rising early the next morning, Haaken felt refreshed after a hot shower. He stood at the mirror and lightly trimmed his short beard as he thought about Layla.

Returning to the bedside, he sat down to plan the day as best he could. After half an hour he got up to make his breakfast meeting with the old man, Henry, from reception. *Time to go and see what information he might have for me.* Making sure his knife and tomahawk were in place, he picked up his backpack, locked up, and headed downstairs to the dining room.

Upon entering he found the old man already seated at a table with a window view of the street outside.

"Morning, Henry," he said, "I trust you are well?"

"Fine, thank you Haaken, please take a seat. Breakfast will be along shortly.'

Haaken took a seat opposite the old man at the table.

"So..." he said, "Where do we start?"

The old man smiled as the kitchen door opened with a creak.

"In a moment, Haaken," he said "here comes our coffee and breakfast. I hope you like bacon and eggs."

There was silence while the two men ate the food and drank their coffee. Once the plates were cleared and fresh cups poured, Haaken pushed his chair back a little to stretch his legs and quietly lit his first Cohiba of the day. Inhaling the smoke and pleasant aroma, he stared at the old man through the smoke. Henry smiled, nodded his head, and spoke.

"Just like your father.." he said "Breakfast and a cigar."

"Okay," said Haaken, "Now tell me more about my father"

The old man eased himself into a comfortable position on his chair and began to talk.

"Your father and I spent many years working together as contractors at the old gold mine up the road out of town. In the end, it became too difficult and costly to continue the mining. In fact, we were partners in our venture, until we were laid off that is."

The old man stared out of the window and continued.

"We were really good friends back then. During the time Harry spent here, he and my sister spent a lot of their spare time together. Your father would be here for several weeks, then disappear and then return again. I did discover from Harry that he had bought a large piece of timberland in the mountains near Solitude. He said he was building a home there."

Drinking some more coffee, Henry continued,

"Well obviously one thing led to another with Delilah and she got pregnant. Trying to do the honourable thing, I told your father he had to marry her. But he refused. Needless to say, we got into a fight, which my sister stopped, and then we all sat down to talk it through. But from then on our friendship was never the same. It was then your father confided in us that he had access to his own gold."

Henry shifted a little uncomfortably on his chair before saying,

"He told us he had found a mine. A rich one at that. He said we were not to fret about Delilah being pregnant and not having a husband. He said he would take care of us all. Well, Delilah got really upset with that comment and left in a storm of anger and headed to one of the bars in town. Let me just tell you my sister is a serious alcoholic. Always has been since she was a teenager. Harry then told me some more about this rich deposit of gold. He showed some of it to me. I asked him where from but your father just smiled and told me not to worry. Said he would take care of everything."

Haaken adjusted himself as he was getting a little numb from the hard wooden chair.

"Got any more coffee, Henry?" he said.

Henry ordered a fresh pot for their table.

"So..." said Haaken, "What happened with your sister's pregnancy?"

Henry continued,

"Your father kept his word and made sure Delilah was well looked after right up to the time she gave birth. But it was about three months after when he disappeared. We received no more money after that. It became my responsibility to look after my sister and her kids."

The old man had become agitated and angry. Haaken stared at him while he took a sip of coffee and relit his Cohiba. He drew deeply and slowly and let the smoke trickle out of his nostrils.

"What happened then?"

Henry took a deep breath, calmed down, and continued.

"Delilah began to drink and smoke herself into a stupor," he said. "I heard she was leaving the babies at home while she went out to drink and find men in bars. I went down to our house to see for myself. I was living here at the Hotel and still do. It was only when I got there, that I found out that one child was missing. Only her baby daughter was in the crib. I went off to find Delilah and get her home."

Pausing for some more coffee, Henry continued.

"I found her drunk out of her mind with some idiot at the bar. Getting her home wasn't easy but I managed. It was only when I got her home and asked her about the whereabouts of her son that I got to know what happened"

The old man reached for more coffee but Haaken stopped him.

"Henry.." he said, "I think it's time for a beer."

Nodding in agreement, Henry called the waitress. There was silence in the room until the drinks were delivered.

Haaken rocked back on his chair, beer in one hand, Cohiba in the other.

"What happened to her son?" he asked quietly.

"Harry took him away from her!" Henry blurted out.

"What the hell?!" said Haaken, the surprise making his voice rumble loudly.

"Yes..." said the old man, "Harry took him from her and left. I tried to get her to tell me what really happened to but all she did was wail and cry that the bastard stole her son. Furthermore, no-one ever saw your father or my sister's son again."

"Wait a minute!" said Haaken "Are you saying your sister had twins?"

"Yes she did..." said Henry looking directly at Haaken with a strange look of triumph in his eyes, "A boy and a girl. Their names are Morana and Ulfred."

Haaken's eyes opened wide in shock as he brought the front legs of his chair crashing to the wooden floor with a resounding thump. Leaning aggressively towards Henry he spoke between clenched teeth,

"What exactly are you saying, Henry?" he said in a quiet deadly tone, "My brother's name is Ulfred!"

Henry quickly looked away and nervously called for two more beers. Looking into Haaken Hunter's angry eyes was not a pleasant experience.

When the beers arrived Haaken drank half down and put the glass down on the table with a sharp thud. Haaken studied Henry's watery old eyes as they blinked nervously back at him. *What are you up to old man? Why that strange look earlier?*

Lighting up what was left of his Cohiba, Haaken slowly exhaled a large cloud of smoke across the table while the old man began to fidget.

"You're telling me that Ulfred is not my twin brother.," he said in a low voice.

"Yes I am..." said Henry "He's not your twin brother. Ulfred is your stepbrother. He is the true twin to Morana, my sister's daughter. You all have the same father, but your mother and their mother are two different people."

"Well, I'll be damned. The horny old bastard!" said Haaken, slapping the table suddenly with a large hand as the smoke drifted slowly across the table from his Cohiba "Order some more beer, Henry!"

The old man happily obliged as he had feared that the news would cause Haaken to beat him to a pulp.

As the order arrived, Henry was called away to deal with some guests and a problem with the sewerage system.

"We'll talk again, Haaken," said Henry as he stood to leave.

"We most certainly will!" growled Haaken "Henry! What is your last name?"

"It's Renwick..." said the old man as he walked away.

Haaken's eyes narrowed to slits as he watched Henry disappear from the dining room. *Coincidence? I think not!*

Normally Haaken would smoke one, or half of one of his Cohiba Black Pequeños per day, but today was an exception. Lighting up a fresh smoke, he sat staring through the dining room window at the street outside and mulled over everything he had just heard.

CHAPTER FOURTEEN

The Note.

After questioning her mother and discovering that she had a twin brother, Morana Renwick had headed up to her own cabin at the old mine just out of town. She sat quietly at her writing bureau with a frown upon her beautiful face. She had read and re-read the contents of the note from her loving Uncle Henry.

My dear Morana

You will receive a package containing the key to great wealth - gold. Along with the key, there is a map showing you where to find this gold. However, this map is missing some vital details. You will need to accomplish the following to be able to secure this wealth for our family. I have been watching you grow your whole life and it is now time for you to secure what is rightfully ours. I am certain that you, and you alone have the necessary will to accomplish this. You already have the mines assay and gold claims manager under your control. He must change the claim from the double H mine (Harry Hunter) into the name of H&D (Henry &Delilah). This is necessary for us to sanctify the date from that period. Naturally, you will own your mother's share. Once the claim documentation is secure, you will have to find the exact location of this mine. As I already said, I have watched you all your life and I know you are capable of getting the information you will need, no matter what it takes.

The Hunter brothers owe us this wealth, Morana. Their father, Harry, lied to me back then and took something of ours. He left us with nothing. You will need to question the Hunter brothers for the details and location of the mine.

I will be in touch,

Your ever-loving uncle

Henry.

Morana stared down at the note while a cesspool of twisted thoughts swirled through her mind. She lifted the heavy gold nugget and rubbed it slowly and sensuously with her fingers. Morana could almost taste the power and wealth the gold would bring. Now, with the promise of it so conveniently at her fingertips, her eyes glittered with greed as her thoughts gathered momentum.

I have Ulfred. Now I must get from him the details of the mine site. Yes, Harry Hunter, you stole my heritage. I will have it back. Mine. All of it will be mine! And Uncle Henry doesn't realise that I know who Ulfred is. Morana gloated to herself, feeling her desire growing as she closed her eyes and envisaged the untold wealth and power the gold would bring.

A low growl from her Rotweiller, Demon, alerted her to movement from Ulfred. Lashing the dog with her riding crop, Morana hissed with a frightful scowl upon her face.

"Shut up you dumb animal!"

The poor dog cowered away from her, not sure which way to look. Morana turned to look at Ulfred. She noted he was still unconscious from the sleeping drug he had ingested with the glass of water. She walked over to look down on Ulfred, as a horrible plan began to form in her mind. A sadistic smile began to tug at her full lips, her tongue flicked out to lick them, leaving a wet sheen that enhanced the lustful look on her face. Quietly walking over to her writing bureau, Morana retrieved a small syringe and a vial of Ketamine from one of the drawers.

She returned to stand over Ulfred, her breathing a little faster now, in anticipation of what was to come. Prodding him quite hard in the neck with her forefinger produced a weak grunt. *Good, he is still fast asleep.* Morana drew 10mg of Ketamine into the syringe and stabbed the needle into Ulfred's neck, slowly pushing the plunger down and taking her time to empty its contents into him. *I don't want to cause a brain haemorrhage just yet do I?* Licking her lips again, she knew he would soon be unconscious for at least an hour.

Morana left the room and went outside to the small garden tool shed just outside the kitchen. Once there she set about looking for something sharp, humming happily to herself as she rummaged about the shelves. When she saw it her

eyes lit up with excitement and with a small squeal of delight, she picked up a heavy pair of pruning shears. Although the curved blades were covered lightly with rust, the cutting edges were still razor sharp. Quickly returning to the cabin, she walked briskly into the warm lounge and over to the now totally unconscious Ulfred.

She carefully pulled his left arm out from under the blanket covering him. Morana's face was now suffused with blood lust. Her eyes had a maniacal glint to them, while her chest rose up and down rapidly in anticipation as she reached down and gently extended his forefinger with the snarling Wolf's head ring. She did so to make space for the curved pruning shears blades.

Picking up the shears, she carefully released the holding clip to let the blades spring open like a hungry bird's beak. Moving slowly in a calm sensuous, almost loving way, she slid the lower curved blade under his finger.

Closing her eyes in the pure ecstasy of the moment, she slowly squeezed the shears shut. The sharp but slightly rusted curved blades sliced easily into the flesh of the finger, meeting some resistance as they closed onto the bone. Her knuckles turned white with tension as her powerful hands clenched tightly around the handles to close the sharp blades with a small crunching sound similar to munching on a mouthful of dry corn flakes. The severed finger almost separated from Ulfred's hand in one movement. Still gripping the handles tightly closed, Morana was having a little difficulty tugging on an obstinate piece of skin before the finger came free and dropped onto the blanket.

Opening her eyes, she looked down at the severed finger where it had fallen on the blanket, the freshly severed nerves made it twitch as if still attached to his hand. The snarling Wolf's head ring on it, now spattered with blood appeared to glare at her in anger. Panting heavily, Morana let out a groan of pure pleasure, as she watched Ulfred's hand pump out spurts of blood from the torn bloody stump of where his finger used to be.

Dropping the shears to the floor, she walked back to the kitchen and returned with a small medical bag, a hand blow torch, and a large metal salad spoon. From the medical bag, she retrieved a bandage, some cotton wool, and wound seal powder. Seating herself comfortably next to Ulfred, she applied a tourniquet to his wrist. Once the bleeding had almost stopped, she lit the small blow torch which stood on the small side table where she had placed it. Her eyes revelling in the bright blue flame hissing away from the nozzle, she happily began to heat the spoon.

When it was red hot, Morana picked up his hand, and using the inside curve of the spoon started cauterizing the stump. Sliding the smooth red hot spoon over and around the stump, stopping once to reheat the spoon, she sealed the wound around the slightly splintered but otherwise evenly cut bone. With eyes focused intently on the raw stump, she hummed quietly to herself with an insane but radiant smile upon her beautiful face. She relished the scent of burnt flesh and hot bone as the red hot spoon slid easily over the mutilated flesh, sealing it over the exposed bone.

Once the finger stump was cauterized, Morana took a little time to admire her handiwork. A fine sheen of sweat covered her face. Still panting from her highly aroused state, her body tensed and shook with unbridled pleasure. Morana let out a deep sigh of satisfaction and liberally shook wound powder over her handiwork. Then she carefully bound a crisp new bandage several times around Ulfred's mutilated hand to neatly cover the amputation.

With a satisfied smile, Morana carried the tools of her sadistic surgical amputation back to the kitchen. After thoroughly cleaning and rinsing off the pruning shears, she returned them to the tool shed, neatly placing them back on the shelf. She then went back into the kitchen to put the rest of the items away.

Returning to the lounge, she collected the severed finger and ring, placed them in a plastic bag, and put them in the freezer. Ulfred had begun to moan and whimper as the pain from his savagely amputated and roughly cauterized finger stump began to register on his slowly returning conscious mind. The Ketamine was starting to wear off. Morana carefully injected him with some more, her ugly mind thinking rapidly about where to place Ulfred for a more intimate question and answer session.

Quietly drinking a fresh cup of coffee, she sat scheming for a short while. *I must get the information about the mine from him soon. Now, how do I get his brother here? Hmm.. Yes! I've got it!*

Getting up to check on Ulfred, she found him still out for the count. *Whoops! I must have given him a little more than I thought - looks like he won't be coming out of it for at least another hour or so.*

Morana summoned Ozil to the cabin on the telephone. As soon as he answered his phone, she barked loudly,

"Ozil, get up to the cabin now!"

Soon after, the sound of a vehicle skidding to a stop announced Ozil's arrival. Morana quickly went outside via the kitchen with Ulfred's bloody finger and ring now wrapped in a grubby cloth. Before Ozil could get out of his vehicle, she approached his window and handed the package to him.

Reaching out to take it, Ozil let out a small shriek of horror as he clutched the bloody cloth,

"Morana, what have you done?"

"Don't be such a baby! I want you to take this and give it to Haaken Hunter, Ulfred's brother. Go to their homestead and tell him you found it nailed to your office door. Ask him where Ulfred is, it will confuse him. Tell him you want Ulfred, he has something of yours. Okay? I want him here!"

Still staring at the bloody cloth with a pale face, Ozil simply nodded his head.

"Here, take this paper, I've written basic directions to get there. If you have to stop and ask directions, do so. I want him here quickly. Now go, and you better take some help with you."

Ozil started his vehicle and left in a hurry for the Hunter Homestead.

Morana stared after the disappearing vehicle deep in thought. Her evil mind thinking of the perfect place to move Ulfred so she could continue to unleash more sadistic torture on his body. It came to her quickly. *I know! The room off the main mine tunnel will be perfect! Now, how can I move him?*

Casting her eyes about the big open yard, they came to rest on a large empty old metal explosives box sitting atop a long-handled four-wheeled cart. It had a front axle for pulling and turning the cart. *That will do perfectly!*

Taking the cart to the room inside the mine, Morana pushed the large metal explosives box off it onto the concrete floor. She pulled the cart all the way back to the kitchen door and turned it around, ready for the journey towards the old mine entrance across the yard. Suddenly she abruptly changed her crazed mind. *No! That won't work. I have to get the cart next to him.* She quietly walked back into her lounge to check on Ulfred. *Good, he is still unconscious.* Returning to the cart outside the kitchen door, Morana carefully eased the cart through the wide kitchen door into the kitchen. *Good thing I had the cabin made with extra-wide doorways.* She pulled the cart into the large lounge and wheeled it around to park up tightly next to the couch. She reached across the bed of the cart with a stretch and grabbed the far side of the blanket wrapped around Ulfred. Morana pulled it firmly towards her. As the blanket came, it effectively rolled the unconscious naked body neatly onto the flat steel bed of the cart. It was just long enough to take the length of his body. Fortunately Ulfred was a slim fellow and not very tall. Morana covered him with the blanket and hauled his body from the cabin across the yard towards the room in the old mine tunnel.

Morana Renwick was exceptionally strong for her size. Even so, she was sweating profusely as she hauled Ulfred up the slope towards the mine entrance. Glaring angrily at him lying on the cart, she ground out through clenched teeth.

"Oh, my dear twin brother, you are going to pay dearly for this."

About halfway there, the Rottweiler, Demon, suddenly took it upon himself to worry a corner of blanket trailing on the ground to one side of the cart. With a deep growl, he bit down on the blanket, vigorously shaking his head, he pulled it right off Ulfred's naked body and ran off.

Dropping the cart handle, Morana, already in a highly psychotic state of pure hatred and festering anger, completely lost it and went berserk. Snatching up her riding crop from where she had tucked it securely under Ulfred's shoulder, she chased after the dog screaming loudly.

"Demon! You useless piece of shit! I'll kill you!"

Demon looked up at the insane spectacle of Morana rapidly bearing down on him brandishing the riding crop. At the sight of her face, a twisted ugly mask of glaring hatred, he immediately dropped the blanket and cowered away from her. But it was too late. She laid into the poor dog mercilessly until he lay there torn and bleeding on the ground. Still seething with rage, Morana uncermoniously dragged the dog by its hind legs into the mine to a point some distance down the main tunnel where she padlocked him tightly with a chain around his neck to an old steel ring in the tunnel wall. Obviously, she had done this many times

before. She kicked the dog as it lay in a pool of bloody water on the tunnel floor atop the worn steel rail lines that disappeared deep into the mine.

"Useless dumb animal! You can lay here and die!"

The job done, she stomped off to retrieve the blanket and get the cart. Finally, after much effort, she managed to manoeuvre the cart into the room off the main tunnel. She paused for a moment in the room with its overhead fluorescent lighting. The walls were painted a stark white which glared painfully bright under the lights.

Morana pulled the cart to a stop next to the large steel explosive box. The box was the same length as the cart and deep enough to take Ulfred's body. It lay, with the lid open on the floor, supported by two planks running crosswise under each end. Removing the blanket to reveal Ulfred's stark white naked body, Morana crossed over to a steel workbench to retrieve a stinking canvas bag and a foul looking ball of filthy cloth. Skirting a strange looking chair in the middle of the floor, she returned to the cart.

She stood for a moment looking down at Ulfred's battered face with a strange look of anticipation on her face. Then she reached down to force his jaw open and plunged the filthy ball of cloth into his mouth before securing the bag tightly around his head. After tightly binding his hands and feet, Morana nodded her head with a satisfied smile as she admired her handiwork. The unconscious Ulfred now resembled a pale naked hooded man awaiting some kind of weird human sacrificial ceremony.

With much exertion, pushing and grunting a little, she managed to get Ulfred lying on his back in the bottom of the steel box before slamming it closed and securing the lock. She then took a length of chain and ran it around the box a couple of turns and padlocked it. Smiling happily, she left the room, locking the steel door behind her. Then returned to her cabin to prepare. Already she could feel her lust rising as she thought through her plans. *First a nice cup of coffee and a hot shower to freshen up. Then I'll have a nice chat with Ulfred Hunter.*

CHAPTER FIFTEEN

Delilah

After hearing Henry's startling revelations about his father, Haaken sat quietly in the Hotel dining room for a full hour. When the old man did not reappear, he decided it was time to take a look at Ozil's movements.

Returning briefly to his room to retrieve his long waterproof winter coat, he slipped quietly from the hotel. He pulled the large hood over his head as he emerged from the revolving door. *Now, nobody will recognize me ambling along the sidewalk in the winter chill.*

Recalling the directions that Layla had given him the night before, Haaken made his way towards Delilah's house. Several streets and a few blocks away from the hotel, Haaken found the house. Layla's description had been perfect. It was the only lime green house with black pitch roof tiles on the street. Walking on the opposite side of the street he watched to see if there were any lights on or signs of activity in the house.

Not seeing any sign of occupation, he decided to have a closer look. Moving quietly up the open drive, he walked past the front porch to the rear of the house. Peeking through the kitchen window, there was no sign of anyone inside.

Okay. He thought. *I'll try the door... here goes.* Slowly turning the handle he pulled at it gently. He raised his eyebrows in mild surprise as the door opened without a squeak. Easing himself into the kitchen, he gently closed the door behind him. Stopping briefly there, Haaken was impressed. He had never seen a kitchen as clean as this. Taking a short step forward he froze as the sound of a heavy cough laden with loose phlegm came from the open door to the adjoining room. Slowly crossing the floor to the door, he peered around the door jamb to see who was in the next room. Across the room, lying on a couch was a terrible sight to see. Haaken could not believe his eyes. There on the couch was the source of the tortured breathing. An old woman languished there, the wheezing sound of her chest heaving laboriously as she sucked in what little air she could and just as quickly expelled the air with a wet bubbling sound. The smell of alcohol and cigarette smoke permeated the air in the lounge which was already tainted with wood smoke from the fireplace. Haaken recoiled from the door in shock. *Holy shit! That must be Delilah. I wonder if I could get her to talk?*

So intent was Haaken on watching the old woman that he failed to hear the person approaching the front door until the sound of a key grating in the lock caught his attention.

Shit! Better get out of here! As he turned quietly away, his knee joint popped with a loud clicking sound.

The old woman weakly lifted up her head to see what had made the strange noise. She saw his face peering at her around the side of the kitchen doorway. Her eyes widened in fright and she immediately began to shriek loudly in a strange, emphysema-laden cacophony of wheezes and wet bubbling sounds.

"Harry!" she yelled weakly "You bastard! You stole my baby!"

Haaken stared in disbelief at the open toothless maw of the haggard woman. Her wispy grey hair in wild disarray, standing out from her head in every direction. Her head collapsed back onto the pillow that supported her as the sound of the front door crashing open announced Ozil's arrival.

"Mom! Are you okay?" the nasal sound of his voice called out.

Haaken left the kitchen as quickly and quietly as he could with his heart pounding heavily in his chest from the shocking sight of Delilah. Pulling the door firmly closed behind him, he quickly disappeared around the side of the house and down the street.

Stopping some distance from the away, he grinned nervously to himself as the vision of the old woman's face made him wince.

Fucking hell, that woman could scare the bejesus out of a ghost!

Reaching for a Cohiba with a slightly shaking hand he lit up and walked on back towards The Slaughtered Lamb for a beer. *I'll have to rethink getting my hands on Ozil. Most likely the warehouse will be a better place for a quiet chat with him.*

CHAPTER SIXTEEN

All Tied Up

Pain! Such dreadful pain! Emanating in pulsating white hot waves from the nerve endings of the stump where his severed finger used to be. It grew and grew in intesity until it forced him from his unconscious state.

A tortured groan of discomfort escaped his dry lips.

Ulfred began to come to, as savage pins and needles stabbed relentlessly through his arms and legs making him groan a little louder this time.

More pain from the stump on his hand, tightly bound wrists and feet, as he struggled for air while gagging on the stinking, foul-tasting cloth stuffed into his mouth. He could smell and feel the roughness of some kind of oily hood or wrapping about his head.

His mind screamed silently and somewhat irrationally, *Holy shit, my circulation is being cut off.* His body jerked suddenly with an involuntary spasm, making him bump his head hard against something solid and metallic in front of him. *Shit!*

He opened his eyes, seeing nothing but darkness. When he tried to yell, he could only make a feeble choking noise through the stinking gag while his mind screamed out. *Where the fuck am I?*

The pain raged from his left hand, being driven to excruciating levels from the pins and needles in his bound limbs. *Dear God in heaven, why is my hand so fucking sore?*

Shaking his head slowly from side to side as he tried to clear his mind, Ulfred knew the truth. *You really screwed up this time buddy!*

Trying to think was damn nigh impossible, with the raging thirst dominating his mind he gagged dryly several times against the foul stinking horrible tasting cloth wedged into his mouth. *Water! Dear God, I need some water!*

The dire need for water was suddenly swept away, when, from outside his confined cell of darkness, the sound of approaching footsteps intruded into his oxygen-starved mind and came to an abrupt stop close by. Sudden silence followed and he strained his neck in the confined space in an effort to pick up even the slightest sound.

For what seemed an eternity, only absolute silence filled the darkness with a suffocating presence. Ulfred flinched as abruptly the silence was loudly broken by the metallic jangling of a chain being dragged across the outside of his dark box-like prison. He tried to shout but nothing came out. Only a dry croak issued from his throat, deadened by the foul gag.

Suddenly, the obstruction in front of his head was moved out of the way with the tortured sound of rusty hinges. A breath of cool fresh air washed over him as he breathed deeply through his nose, a huge relief from the hot stale air he had been struggling to breathe. All he could see was darkness with his head covered or wrapped in some kind of thick material impregnated with a foul oily substance.

Still a little groggy from the Ketamine, his nostrils flared open as the wonderful scent of Chanel No 5 mixed beautifully with the fresh air he sucked so greedily into his oxygen-starved lungs. More bursts of pins and needles stabbed excruciating pain through his limbs.

"Oh my poor baby," crooned a sultry voice close to the side of his head.

He felt a hand patting him gently on the top of his head through the hood and despite his terrible condition he felt a subtle stirring in his loins. Her low smoky voice spoke as she caressed his fevered brow. The sound reached far into the depths of his lonely soul like the sirens of old, tempting sailors on the high seas. Ulfred felt truly miserable as he thought to himself. *God help me. She is so beautiful. I can't help myself.*

Her fingers gently pulled the front of the foul stinking hood up far enough to expose his mouth and remove the disgusting gag. Gently, she squirted cool water into his open parched mouth and he gulped greedily. She slowly released the bindings from his feet and hands. Ulfred screamed in agony as blood pumped freely once again. *My hand, my hand, what happened to my hand?* Strong hands reached down to help him stand up and climb out of what he could only assume was some kind of metal box. Trying to stand on weak, wobbly legs, he realized he was still naked as the cold air began to dig its icy fingers into his body. Those same hands guided him and gently placed him on a chair, a strange chair, all cold metal, that felt a bit like a toilet seat to his naked buttocks. Slowly but surely, he was secured firmly to the seat with leather restraints. *What now?* His mind tormented him.

Beginning to shiver from the cold, Ulfred turned his head slowly from side to side, listening intently and trying to figure out how many others were there. His thought process was suddenly interrupted by a wet, smacking sound of something being flicked against the floor in front of him.

What the fuck is making that sound? As the thought formed in his mind, his question was instantly answered.

Pain! Dear God, the pain! Excruciating, mind-numbing and blinding in its intensity, the unbelievable pain tore upwards through every nerve of his body, from his crushed sweaty scrotum which had only a moment ago been hanging through the opening in the toilet like seat and slowly tightening up in the ice-cold air. Any lust that had stirred in his loins vanished in that horrible split second. With his head hanging forward, spittle and blood dribbled from his slackened mouth. Ulfred had almost bitten his tongue through.

Again from somewhere in front of him, another wet-like slap to the floor followed instantly with another crushing blow to his gonads.

Pain! Again! More excruciating agony exploded through his mind, so intense that although his mouth gaped wide in an insane grimace, no sound emerged. His head lolled loosely on his shoulders as consciousness began to recede into the welcome velvety darkness of nothing. Still, somehow far away and deep inside the pained depths of his tortured mind he could hear her guttural groan of deep pleasure. His mind and body lost all thought and any sensation of pain from his hand.

Ice cold water tore his mind abruptly back from the darkness of the unconscious world of nothingness. Again her gorgeous sultry voice gently washed over his wracked body and his mind screamed. *Holy Shit!* Ulfred Hunter tried to breathe. *So much pain! I'm losing it! What the fuck is going on? This mad bitch is trying to kill me!* His thoughts were rambling, dull, and rapidly becoming incoherent. *What? Huh? Fucking hell! What is she saying?*

There was her voice again, heavy with lust, her tone full of sexual promise.

"My poor baby. We can stop this if you just tell me where the gold mine is?" her voice purred in dulcet tones.

Ulfred began to shake violently. The appalling agony from his battered body now going into deep shock was overwhelming. As the warm soft blanket of darkness surrounded him and he finally lost consciousness, there was a vague question in the back of his mind. *What Gold Mine?*

CHAPTER SEVENTEEN

The Warehouse.

Haaken arrived at The Slaughtered Lamb still a little shaken by Delilah's haggard appearance and toothless mouth. Entering quietly, he settled down at the bar. Layla spotted him and quickly walked along to stop in front of him.

"Are you okay? You look like you have just seen a ghost!"

"I feel like I have just seen worse. One look at Delilah's face and I'm convinced a ghost would look more pleasant!"

"Oh dear, does she look that bad now? I haven't seen her for quite a while, not since Morana and Ozil have kept her cooped up in that house."

"I would rather face an angry bear than look at that face again!"

"Careful what you wish for, Haaken!" Layla admonished him with a small frown which made her look even more appealing.

Haaken politely questioned Layla more thoroughly about Ozil's work habits. He discovered that he was quite regular in his habits, leaving the lime green house every morning at about 9.00 am to make his way on foot to the warehouse near the railway station. Apparently, he liked the freshh air.

After spending another pleasant evening with Layla, Haaken returned to the hotel to a restless night's sleep tormented by visions of his brother dying somewhere. In Haaken's mind, Ulfred would always be his one and only brother no matter what anyone else said or proved otherwise. *If anyone is going to reprimand Ulfred or give him a good clout, it will be me. God help anyone who harms or abuses my brother in any way. They will answer to me!*

Rising early, he took a cold shower to get his blood flowing and clear his mind. Not feeling particularly hungry, he quietly left the Hotel and headed on foot for the old warehouse. Once there he found a good vantage point from which to observe the entrance. Rubbing his hands to warm them in the chill of the morning, he settled down to wait. Sure enough, Ozil appeared in the distance, ambling along with a slight limp : the after effect of having Morana's pointed shoe, kick him between his buttocks the previous morning. Haaken watched Ozil unlock the smaller door set into the large sliding main doors of the warehouse and disappear inside.

Patiently waiting a good two minutes, Haaken emerged from his hidden vantage point behind a large double dumpster at the corner of the warehouse next door to the one Ozil had entered. He quickly made for the entrance door. Very slowly and as quietly as he could, he opened the door and slipped inside. He padded softly along the sidewall still in deep shadow, looking around the warehouse. The daylight from the pale rising winter sun filtering in through the filthy windows high up on the steel walls only managed to dimly light the far side of the building and part of the ground floor. In the dim light, he could make out a set of steel stairs rising up to a wide mezzanine floor with two large offices strategically placed on top of it.

In times past they obviously let the factory managers observe the floor from there. The sad state of disrepair allowed Haaken to blend in with the dark shadows as he moved closer to the stairs, pausing there to look for any other movement. Haaken felt sure that Ozil had gone upstairs to one of the offices. Now all he had to do was proceed up the stairs without making any noise.

Placing one foot on the first step, Haaken carefully tested it with more weight. Luckily it did not creak or make any other noise to betray his arrival. Stealthily, in the way a cat slowly advances on its prey, Haaken finally gained the mezzanine floor. Ready for instant action if one of the office doors suddenly opened, he moved silently towards the door on his right. There he paused to listen. Hearing nothing, he reached out and slowly turned the door handle, opening it a little to peer inside. But only silent darkness greeted him. Flicking on his small pencil torch with its searching beam, Haaken discovered he was looking into a toilet and shower room.

A slight rustle of clothing on skin alerted Haaken to movement behind him. Instantly going into a cat-like spin and crouching down to draw his boot blade, Haaken saw a large wooden club rapidly descending towards his head. Swiftly raising an arm to ward off the blow, he managed to absorb some of the club's impetus as it savagely came down on his wrist and temple. Briefly, Haaken registered a pair of ferret-like eyes as Ozil wielded the heavy club again. He parried the club with the blade, managing to slide the sharp blade along the club to slice into Ozil's fingers. Ozil screamed in agony, instantly dropping the club. The sound of running feet faded into the distance as Haaken groggily attempted to clear his mind before passing out.

Haaken's eyes opened, and for a second or two he wondered where he was. He rapidly moved into a defensive crouching position, still clutching his knife as he recalled the club and arm descending on him. *That little rat almost smashed my head in! I didn't even hear him coming. I wonder what alerted him to my presence.*

Haaken quietly stood up, checked his blade. *Good! I cut the bastard!! Must have been his footsteps I heard running away.* Slowly he wiped the blade clean, before sliding it back into his boot and picking up the club from where Ozil had dropped it.

Turning his attention to the other office, he entered it to find no-one there. Ozil had obviously been the only person to come in today. Something must have alerted him to Haaken's presence on the mezzanine floor. *Damn! Missed the little ferret! Aha!* Haaken now spotted the small red flashing light above the door on the inside wall. *Must be a sensor on the stairs or somewhere covering the floor area. I'm getting rusty. You idiot, wake up! You could have had him, now he's gone!* Rubbing his wrist and gently feeling the welt on his temple, Haaken cast his eyes about the office, looking for any clues to Ulfred's whereabouts and possibly locate Ozil again. He spent a good twenty minutes searching the desk drawers, on top of the large safe and several shelves. He checked the safe handle and found it securely locked. Returning to the large office desk, Haaken started paging through the notepads on the desk, painstakingly examining each page. Several minutes later, he came across a hastily scrawled note. He had found Morana's instructions to Ozil about the package which Ulfred was to deliver personally to her cabin up at the old mine near Goregate.

CHAPTER EIGHTEEN

Closing In

Haaken left the warehouse and headed for The Slaughtered Lamb to see Layla although it wasn't yet opening time. After knocking loudly on the bar door for a few seconds he heard Layla shouting from within.

"Hold your horses, I'm coming!" she cried.

The angry rattle of the key in the door was followed by the sudden opening of it as she thrust her head out to yell some abuse. This quickly changed to a smile as she spoke.

"Oh! It's you, come on in."

After closing and locking the door, Layla followed Haaken over to the bar, where she noticed the large swollen bruise running from his right temple down to his cheekbone.

"Shit, Haaken" she said with alarm "are you okay?"

When she gently reached up to touch his bruised face, he cautiously drew back from her advancing fingers.

"What happened?"

"I went for a quiet chat with Ozil at the warehouse and got jumped by the slippery little ferret. I never heard him sneak up on me. He tried to kill me with a wooden club."

Haaken knew he needed to get going up to the cabin at the old mine out of town fast if he was to have any chance of catching up to Ulfred. Layla turned towards the back of the bar.

"Follow me to the kitchen," she said in a tone that brooked no argument.

Haaken meekly followed her, slowly sliding onto the bench seat at the large wooden kitchen table.

Layla set down a large glass of homemade lemonade and a cup of hot coffee. Haaken grabbed up the glass, drinking the lemonade down in one long swig.

"Thank you, Layla" he said "I didn't realize how much I needed that."

He reached for the coffee while pulling out a fresh Cohiba. Lighting it up, he took a long draw, slowly letting the fragrant smoke trickle from his mouth with closed eyes.

"Haaken, I need to put this ice pack on that bruise!" said Layla approaching him with a determined look on her face.

Haaken opened his eyes in alarm as she advanced with an outstretched arm and ice pack.

"Whoa! Layla take it easy with that ice." he said as he began to ease himself along the bench seat.

Layla did not slow down till she got to his side and then reached up and gently placed the ice against his bruised face. The cold ice on the swollen cheekbone and temple felt better than he thought it would. After a minute or two, he pulled away from the ice pack, turned his swollen face to look directly at Layla, and spoke.

"Do you know where the old mine is?" he asked.

"Sure I do. It's only a few miles out of town, further up the mountain. Why do you ask?" she replied looking at him with a concerned expression on her face.

"I need to get there. I think that's where Ulfred might be"

"You are not going on your own" she said instantly "I'm coming with you."

"No Layla, that's not a good idea,"

"Look at what happens to you when you are on your own!" she said angrily "Your face tells the story."

With a calmer voice, Haaken spoke.

"There will most likely be some serious trouble up there. I would hate it if something were to happen to you."

"I am more than capable of taking care of myself, Haaken!" she said "I am coming with you. End of story!"

Looking into her eyes, he could see she had made her decision.

"Ok..." He said with a smile while thinking she looked quite lovely standing there with a small pout on her lips.

"What about the bar?" he asked.

"I have a stand-in for when I'm not here."

"Well, that's decided then" he said standing up "We need to get going now…"

They locked up the bar after Layla had organized her stand-in manager and walked down the street to the vehicle parked outside the hotel. He opened the passenger door for her before proceeding around to the driver's side and they headed slowly out of town. Their progess was watched by a pair of watery old eyes. Henry was wiping down one of the dining room tables when the Bronco's V8 coughed into life. The old man watched them leave.

Not far out of town they began to drive up the narrow winding road that led up to the old mine. As they rounded a wide bend into a long straight stretch of road, Haaken noticed tire skid marks on the surface and slowed down to a crawl. He followed the skid marks until they disappeared off the road, over the side of a ravine.

Both of them spotted the overturned pickup at the bottom of the shallow ravine. Looking at each other in alarm, they spoke almost simultaneously.

"That's his truck, it's Ulfred's truck!"

Jumping from the Bronco, they scrambled down the shallow ravine to the wreck. Walking slowly around the pickup to examine it, Haaken got down on all fours to peer inside the cab.

"I wonder where he went" he said "There doesn't appear to have been any massive blood loss."

Layla was standing a little way off, with her hands to her mouth as she stared in shock at the damage. Replying in a small tight voice, she spoke.

"He must have got out and somehow made it back up to the road."

Getting to his feet, Haaken nodded in agreement. He slowly cast his eyes across the rocky bottom of the ravine from the stream running under the pickup all the way back up to the road. Then, as he scanned back down the ravine slope, he saw the first sign.

Haaken recognized the telltale stone marker. He remembered how as youngsters, he and Ulfred had used stones or broken dry twigs and leaves to point out something of interest or things they had hidden in the forests and rocky mountainsides of their homestead.

This marker was pointing at something in or around the cab area of the truck. Getting down on all fours again, Haaken peered intently at the ground and open door area of the cab.

Layla had begun to walk around the area to see if anything else might be of help but stopped what she was doing when Haaken raised his hand, motioning her to stand still. She watched him with a quizzical look.

Haaken's face was intense and a serious frown creased his brow as he studied the area immediately in front of him in minute detail. Then he spotted the markings scratched on the door frame near the door locking mechanism. The frown around his eyes and on his forehead deepened as he tried to make out the upside-down words. Then he read them aloud.

"II Duplex Aurum Meum..." he said "And several numbers in Roman numerals."

"What did you say?" asked Layla.

"It's Latin for Double H Gold Mine and what looks like a partial GPS location," he replied.

"Where is Double H Mine?" asked Layla.

"It's my father's secret mine and from the GPS numbers it looks like it it's up in the mountain area near our homestead."

"Latin and Roman numerals?" quizzed Layla.

"Yup, we both had to learn Latin." said Haaken with a wry grin "My father said we would benefit from it. Something about organizing our minds in an orderly way. Anyway, he had an ancient edition of The Public Schools Latin Primer by Benjamin Hall Kennedy printed in eighteen something if my memory serves me correctly. We used to have it drummed into our heads for a couple of hours daily"

"Latin!" replied Layla with a little giggle "Who would have thought that would come in handy?"

Haaken looked into Layla's eyes and chuckled at her light mockery of the ancient language.

Then, with a more serious look, he studied the ground and began to move slowly towards the side of the ravine leading up to the road. After several short steps, he paused and pointed upwards to the roadside.

"Look there" he said pointing upwards "You can see the drag marks from him hauling himself up to the road."

Layla could see the marks now that Haaken had pointed them out to her and she followed him slowly back up to the road. After some exertion and slipping and sliding several times they gained the roadside near the parked Ford Bronco.

Haaken got down into a half-crouch, scanning the ground to the left and right before getting back on his feet.

"Looks like he was lying about here," he said pointing to an area where the soil and debris were still depressed.

He squatting down once again to looked more closely at the damp ground.

"Also appear to be footprints of one other person. Another person and a large dog, judging by the size of the paw prints."

"Perhaps they were helping him," offered Layla.

"Hmm, maybe," replied Haaken quietly.

"You may be right it does look like they got him up. I can see where his feet dragged along the ground for a bit. Then they appear to stagger onwards. I think it must have been a strong person judging by the extra depth of their footprints as they supported him."

"Where do you think they took him?" asked Layla, looking nervously at the surrounding trees.

"Up there..." Haaken muttered while staring up the road into the distance.

He suddenly felt a great unease. A quiet worry and wondering at just what trouble Ulfred had got involved in. Turning to Layla with a small smile, he walked back to the Bronco and she kept pace by his side. Layla could see the worry in his eyes despite his smile and the air of confidence he exuded. Glancing up at him, she wanted to take his hand in hers and offer him some comfort. But she was still unsure, even a little wary and nervous about how he would react.

He seemed to sense her thoughts as he turned his head to look down at her. Layla smiled back, a slight blush rising up her neck and face. She felt then as if he had read her thoughts.

Back at the vehicle, Haaken paused to check his backpack. Quietly fishing around in the bag, he pulled out a fierce-looking 10-inch drop point Bowie knife with an ugly brass knuckle guard over the handle. He slid it into a well-worn leather back scabbard. Taking off his well used waterproof overcoat, he strapped the whole assembly securely to his back before pulling the overcoat back on and climbing into the vehicle.

Looking over at Layla, who had been watching the proceedings without a word, he spoke.

"We'll likely run into a heap of trouble up the road. Do you know how to use a rifle?"

"Absolutely" came the reply "Ever since I was about seven years old."

"Good..." he replied taking the rifle from its leather scabbard and handing it over to her "It's fully loaded. If we run into trouble, don't be shy to use it to shoot back. They may try to kill you,"

Layla took the rifle from him and confidently checked the magazine and bolt action.

"I'm ready." she said staring fiercely ahead.

I like this woman more and more each day. He thought as they drove on up the road.

CHAPTER NINETEEN

More Pain!

Ulfred's last thought, *What gold mine?* still echoed in his mind as another ice-cold bucket of water tore him away from the comforting blanket of the unconscious world and back to the reality of agony. The stinking hood covering was roughly pulled from his head, leaving him blinking slowly like a startled owl in the sterile harsh white fluorescent light which reflected off the stark white walls of the rough-hewn chamber.

Where the fuck, am I? His befuddled mind wondered, as his blurred vision began to clear.

A quiet rustle of movement nearby made him flinch. He expected a painful blow of some kind to follow the movement.

"Hush my poor baby," purred her sultry voice, still laden with lust.

Grunting with the effort, Ulfred began to turn his head in her direction. But it was savagely jerked up and back, causing him to choke and gasp. The sudden movement made his mind swirl in a nauseating, dizzying kaleidoscope of colours. Blinking rapidly to clear his vision, her beautiful pale alabaster face seemed to float into view above him.

Her head was cocked over at an angle with a sweet smile on her face as she gazed down upon him.

"Aaarrgh!" he managed to croak as tears streamed from his eyes and spittle dribbled from his lips.

With the speed of a striking snake, Morana thrust her snarling face so close that his eyes went squint before he closed them. Her hot sweet breath washed over his pale face and she hissed.

"Where is the gold mine, Ulfred?"

He tried to shake his head from left to right but found he couldn't with her painfully tight grip on his hair. All he could do was moan up at her again.

"Aaarrgh!" he mouthed with a choking gurgle.

Morana released his head. It fell heavily forward, allowing him to rapidly gulp in some ice cold fresh air. In a ragged hoarse voice, Ulfred gasped out to her.

"Okay! Okay! No more please! I will tell you."

Her face shone with the most beautiful smile,

"Ulfred you poor baby, we could have avoided all this if you had just told me sooner," she crooned in her soft sultry voice.

Morana began to fuss around Ulfred like a mother hen and the wonderful scent of Chanel No5 wafted over him as she released the restraining straps that bound him to the steel chair.

He tried to get up but his legs were too weak. Sobbing in pain, he collapsed face forward on the cold floor in a crumpled heap, trying to draw his legs up into a foetal position. Kneeling down near him, Morana gently raised his head onto her lap, wiping the sweat from his fevered brow with a soft warm hand.

"Ulfred, tell me where the mine is," she purred softly.

"It's on our homestead somewhere above our cabin," he croaked.

Morana slowly poured some water into his dry mouth. Ulfred gulped the water down gratefully.

"Morana, Morana where are you?" Ozil called out loudly.

The sound of his feet rapidly approaching the room announced his hasty arrival followed by desperate banging on the large steel door.

"Open up, Morana, we need to talk urgently!" shouted Ozil.

Placing Ulfred's head gently on the floor, Morana gracefully rose to her feet and walked over to unlock and open the door.

Ozil burst in, only to come to an abrupt stop as he saw Ulfred's battered naked body lying on the floor. His eyes wide in shock and fear, he thought. *You too, you poor bastard. She really is a monster.*

Turning to her he spoke in a quick panicky voice, words running into each other,

"It's Haaken, he nearly caught me at the warehouse, but I got away."

"Slow down, Ozil and tell me what happened," said Morana.

Taking a deep breath, Ozil told her that soon after he got to their office at the warehouse, Haaken had gained access and had got up to the mezzanine floor. Luckily the hidden sensor had alerted him to Haaken's presence. Ozil continued, the words tumbling from his thin mouth as he waved his blood-soaked, bandaged hand about.

"I managed to sneak up behind him and hit him with the wooden club I keep in the office. But he pulled a knife on me and cut me before he fell down."

"Where is Haaken?" asked Morana in a tight angry voice.

With eyes wide open in fear, Ozil swallowed hard before replying,

"I don't know Morana, I ran away after he cut my hand!"

"You stupid fucking idiot!" hissed Morana "If he is not dead, he probably had a good look around the office and for sure, you would have left some clue there for him to figure out where I am. He is probably on his way here now. You stupid prick! You've led him right to us,"

"I'm sorry, Morana." said Ozil as he cowered away in fear.

All the while, Ulfred watched the macabre scene from where he lay shivering on the floor. The brief respite from Morana's clutches had allowed him to try and assess how much damage she had dealt to his battered and pain racked body. The agony from between his legs had dropped a few notches down from excruciating to a pounding, non-stop ache. But it was when he slowly raised his hand to see why the nerves were sending out continuous stabbing bolts of what felt like hot molten lava that shot up his arm to the very core of his brain, that he could not believe what he saw with his own eyes.

Ulfred let out a blood-curdling shriek of pure horror when he saw the bloody bandaged stump of what was left of his forefinger. *Noooo! Fuck me! She chopped off my finger, why, why you demented bitch?!* His mind howled in shared agony with his missing finger and, blissfully, he fainted.

Together Morana and Ozil wrapped Ulfred in a couple of warm blankets after hauling him outside and bundled him into the back of their black SUV. She ran into the cabin to retrieve the gold nugget, the map, and the incomplete coordinates for the mine.

Jumping into the vehicle, Morana instructed Ozil to get going down the old loop road from the mine used by heavy vehicles which bypassed the town of Goregate and joined the main road a short distance to the south.

"Where are we heading?" asked Ozil after several minutes of driving.

"We are going to the Hunter homestead," she answered.

Ozil glanced nervously at her, remembering his last unpleasant experience at the Hunter homestead.

"Where's your dog?" he asked quietly.

"Damn animal just won't listen to me," she snarled in anger.

"What did you do to Demon?"

"Useless beast can rot in the mine for all I care.." she shouted leaning over towards Ozil in a threatening manner. "Why are you asking, Ozil? You looking for more pain?!"

With an involuntary flinch of pure fear, Ozil leaned as far away from her as he could and continued to drive in stony silence.

CHAPTER TWENTY

Morana's Cabin.

❦

Haaken and Layla arrived up at the old mine workings and Morana's cabin soon after after leaving the wrecked pickup in the ravine. Leaping from the Bronco they approached the cabin with caution. Haaken could clearly see the kitchen door had been left wide open. Raising a hand for Layla to stop, he paused to listen for any sign or sound of movement inside. There was nothing.

Indicating to Layla to move forward with him, they quietly entered the kitchen. Stopping just inside the door, Haaken rapidly took stock of what he could see. There was a blood-stained cloth on the draining board next to the sink, a discarded pile of men's clothes on the floor by the sink, and a neatly placed washed coffee mug on the draining board.

He entered the tastefully furnished lounge where the fire was still roaring away casting a comfortable glow of warmth around the room. The lounge area was clean and neat, the only oddity being the untidy open writing bureau on the far side of the lounge. Layla let out a slow whistle of appreciation at the obvious luxury on display.

"Wow!" she said "A real fancy place she built here, Haaken."

"You got that right. But no sign of my brother..." he grunted.

He began to move about the room, stopping at the open writing bureau. Judging by the scattered pieces of paper, someone had been in a hurry. Haaken carefully searched through the bureau, and then surveyed the collection of items he had found. The Ketamine raised his eyebrows, but the note from Henry to Morana was far more interesting. He could feel his anger growing as he read it. There was definitely a plot to take the mine and betray any previous friendship between Henry and his father.

They continued their search outside the cabin. Haaken could not help but notice a large steel door sealing off the entrance to the old mine in the side of the mountain a short distance up from the cabin. Walking over to it they found it slightly open and upon entering, found the tunnel hacked into the mountain.

Haaken produced a small flashlight which clearly lit up the dark gloomy mine tunnel. Off to one side was a small steel door painted white. He walked over to it and pushed it open to reveal a stark white roughly hewn rocky chamber with walls covered in shotcrete. So bright were the fluorescent lights that their eyes took a moment to adjust. Inside the room they found a long narrow steel box with an open lid and a steel commode like chair with leather restraints. Haaken took a closer look, noticing the leather hood lying on the floor and a long thick wet rope heavily knotted at one end. The knotted end, lying under the chair had blood smeared on it. There were more smears of blood inside the box and on the chair and floor. Of particular note were the bloody drag marks across the floor back to the doorway.

"Looks like the sick bastards were interrogating my brother here." Haaken muttered darkly.

"Oh my God!" said Layla, her face pale as she looked around the room.

Both of them could smell the strange mix of Chanel No 5 and urine pervading the air.

"Let's get out of here..." Haaken said quietly through gritted teeth.

Layla followed him out of the room. A low whining sound cut through the ice-cold air in the tunnel. Haaken stopped so suddenly that Layla bumped into him. About to say something, she held her tongue, seeing his hand motioning her to keep quiet.

The sound came again from further inside the mine.

Pointing his small flashlight into the darkness, the beam revealed the old rail lines glistening wetly as they disappeared into the darkness of the tunnel. Again the low whimpering whine came from within.

"Wait here, Layla, while I check that out," said Haaken

as he followed the old rail line.

He hadn't gone far when the beam from his flashlight picked out two eyes shining back at him from the darkness ahead. The sight was followed by a low growl. The hair on the back of Haaken's neck rose at the sound. Stopping where he was, he crouched down and moved the beam of the torch slowly from left to right to try and locate the source of the warning growl ahead. In the freezing darkness he could just make out a dark form lying down. *I don't think it's a bear. Certainly a wounded animal though.* Haaken moved forward very slowly, calling out softly in a low deep reassuring tone. The dark form struggled painfully to its feet with a quiet whimper and another ineffective warning growl. He could now see he was looking at a large black dog.

"Looks like a wounded dog," he called back to Layla.

Still talking quietly, he moved forward calmly to reassure the dog that he was no threat. Eventually he got close to the animal, which was now lying down again. Moving the beam of the torch over the dog he could see it had been severely beaten and was tethered by a rusty chain to the wall of the tunnel. The dog was completely soaked through from the icy water continually dripping from the tunnel roof and was shivering uncontrollably. It was clear the poor animal had been left here for several hours. *Looks like he has been left to die here!* Haaken scowled angrily at the terrible thought.

Calmly, he sat down in a muddy puddle on the floor and slowly extended his hand while talking very quietly to the wounded animal. *What kind of demented, evil person would do this?* His angry mind demanded. The shivering dog kept its head low to the ground, peering up at Haaken through a pair of pained, soulful brown eyes.

"It's okay, easy boy, I'm here to help you," said Haaken in a low, reassuring voice.

The dog sensed that Haaken meant no harm and managed to shuffle forward a little to get closer to him. Haaken laid his hand reassuringly on the large dog's broad head and gently scratched him behind his ears.

"Let's see if we can get this damned chain off, shall we?" said Haaken looking into the dogs pleading eyes.

He felt around the dog's large neck and located a large padlock fastening the chain to its neck.

"Shit!" he said "Okay boy, looks like a bit of a problem getting that open. Let's see if we can work the chain off the wall,"

Haaken got up to follow the chain to a large spike in the wall.

"Layla!" he called out "Please go to my truck and bring me the spade lying in the back."

"Okay," shouted Layla as she quickly left to do as asked.

She returned soon after with the spade and gasped in shock when she saw the dog lying on the wet, muddy floor of the tunnel.

"I noticed a tool store near the cabin backdoor" he said "Please check in there to see if there is a hammer or some bolt cutters."

As she left, Haaken turned to the wall spike and attempted to dig it out the wall, but it was to no avail. There was only a scattering of sparks when the spade struck the wall. Cursing in frustration, he bent down to pat the dog which had cringed away from the noise.

"Sorry buddy, just trying to free you," he said in a calm voice.

He squatted down beside the dog with his hand resting on its broad head and waited for Layla to return with something more substantial. The dog looked up, appearing to understand, and licked Haaken's hand.

Layla returned, struggling with a large sledgehammer. Instinctively she knelt on the floor with her hands on the dog as Haaken began to strike the wall spike with powerful blows in an attempt to loosen it from the wall. After several strikes from the sledgehammer, the aged eye of the rusty spike snapped where it held the chain, releasing it in a noisy clatter on the floor.

The injured dog had not moved once during Haaken's onslaught on the spike. Retrieving the chain, he stooped to pick up the dog with a strained grunt. Haaken stood up, smiled with satisfaction at Layla, then made his way out of the old mine tunnel to his truck. Once there, he gently placed the dog in the back. Reaching into his backpack, Haaken pulled out a bag with pemmican in it and scooped out a handful, which he held under the dog's mouth.

Still keeping a watchful eye on Haaken, the dog gratefully licked up the dried meat from his hand. Patting the dog on the head, Haaken ran his other hand over the dog's flanks and legs to try and feel what damage there was. With a look of instinctive trust, the dog let him proceed while sniffing around for more food.

"Looks like someone beat the hell of you, boy, and then left you to die," muttered Haaken angrily.

The dog was now eagerly sniffing Haaken's hand for more meat and he obliged with another handful of pemmican to be rewarded with a few wags from the dog's stumpy tail. Haaken playfully ruffled the dog's head and scratched it behind its ears. Layla laughed happily at the sight of him and the injured dog bonding.

"I had better have a look in the tool shed for something to get this damn chain off his neck." he said.

Leaving Layla watching the dog, he went to rummage about in the shed. He returned with a triumphant look on his face and an ancient hacksaw with a well-used blade clutched in his hand.

Taking a firm grip on the chain link with the padlock, he proceeded to saw away until, after what felt like an age, the worn blade finally cut through both sides of the link and he was able to remove it from the dog's neck. The large Rottweiler gratefully shook his head, feeling the freedom from the rusty chain that had bound him to the tunnel wall. The dog scrambled to its feet faster than Haaken thought it could and before he could back away, licked him across his face. Haaken chuckled loudly, wiping his face with the back of his hand,

"Easy boy.." he said "You are free to go,"

Haaken waved his hand to encourage the dog to leave the vehicle. The dog jumped down, shook itself, turned around, and sat down looking at Haaken with bright brown eyes. Layla watched both of them with a smile.

"Right..." he said "It's time to leave this horrible place. I think they have taken Ulfred to our homestead to find my father's lost gold mine."

Opening the driver's door, he turned to look down at the dog sitting patiently on the ground. It watching him intently with its large brown eyes. Reaching inside the vehicle Haaken pulled the front seat forward.

"Okay.." he said "Are you coming with?"

Needing no further encouragement, the large dog leapt with alacrity onto the back seat.

"Looks like we made a new friend," Haaken said to Layla as he got behind the wheel "I'm sure they've taken Ulfred with them to find my father's gold mine, which from the coordinates, appears to be somewhere in the mountains above our property. I hope we can catch up."

Turning the vehicle around, they headed back to town.

Once again, a pair of watery old eyes observed Haaken's return to town with Layla as they drove past the Hotel Hope. Pulling up outside The Slaughtered Lamb, they went inside briefly to collect some supplies for the journey ahead. Here Haaken managed to clean the dog and rub him dry with an old towel while it eagerly lapped up a bowl of fresh water.

Returning from the back kitchen with her own backpack, Layla spoke.

"What are you going to call him?" she asked.

The dog lay patiently by Haaken's feet, keeping a watchful eye on every move he made.

"I'm not sure..." he replied "He must answer to something. He seems to respond to my voice when I say hey boy!"

With that, the huge dog immediately lifted his broad head and looked at Haaken. Layla laughed delightedly at the scene in front of her.

"Calling him 'Boy' just won't do Haaken." she said.

"I'll think of a name soon enough. Speaking of soon, we had better get going."

Haaken lit up a fresh Cohiba as they left town, quietly enjoying it while the large, all-terrain tires hummed along on the highway. Layla settled down watching the road ahead as the day got darker, heralding a cold wet night ahead of them.

"Where do you think they are?" asked Layla.

"Some distance down the road ahead" he replied "I just hope that Ulfred is still breathing,"

Haaken flicked on the headlights. They both stared ahead into the night, their ghostly faces illuminated by the reflection of the powerful twin beams of the halogen lights piercing the dark night in front of them as the road sped by beneath the wheels.

CHAPTER TWENTY ONE

The Hunt For The Double H Gold Mine.

The hum of speeding tires on the road and slight bumpiness roused Ulfred from his addled pain-filled state. He could hear her voice cruelly mocking Ozil for being a weak specimen of manhood, and then Ozil's whiny reply. He discovered to his dismay, that they had bound him hand and foot once again. Suddenly Morana's head appeared above him as he lay trussed up in the back of the vehicle. She had clearly heard him moving about. Ulfred looked up into her beautiful eyes. *How can such vile evil, be surrounded by so much beauty?*

"Ulfred.." she said with an innocent smile "You had better know where this mine is. Unless of course you want more pain,"

Keeping his mouth shut, Ulfred began to fret internally. How the hell he was going to convince them he knew where it was? Morana's head disappeared as she turned back to the front.

"Can't you drive faster you imbecile?" she hissed at Ozil.

Ulfred's mind turned to his brother. *Haaken, I hope you are at home my brother, if ever I needed you, I truly need your help now.* With a desperate groan of despair he tried to curl up and ignore the intense pain pulsing up from his mutilated left hand. As darkness fell he floated in and out of consciousness with the words from the song 'You're as cold as ice' playing on a constant, maddening loop in his pain-ridden mind.

Several hours later, the sharp sting of a needle piercing his neck brought his mind briefly back into focus. Ulfred looked up into the dimly lit face of Morana as she pulled the syringe from his skin.

"Can't have you making a noise while we stop for fuel, can we darling?" she said "A little Ketamine for your pain…"

Ulfred felt the vehicle slowing down as he passed out once again.

CHAPTER TWENTY TWO

Gaining Ground.

A slight bump in the road jerked Layla from her restless sleep with her head resting on her folded anorak against the door pillar. Blinking, she looked across to Haaken who from all appearances had not moved an inch since she dozed off. He still stared straight ahead with a fixed and determined look chiselled into his face. Only the trickle of cigar smoke escaping from his mouth and nostrils indicated that he was still breathing. Layla stretched like a cat to wake herself.

"How far are we now?" she asked.

"Still a way to go," he drawled quietly.

Reaching into her backpack she produced two water bottles. Opening both of them, she passed one across to Haaken, who with a polite nod of thanks drank thirstily from it.

"I don't know about you but I need to pee..." said Layla "Are we stopping soon for fuel?"

"No. We are not stopping. I have enough fuel in the long-range tank to get us to my home."

Haaken slowed down and pulled well over off the road in the darkness. He turned in his seat to look at Layla.

"You said you need to pee?"

Layla looked at him for a quiet second.

"Well, if you don't plan on stopping anywhere else, I had better get busy."

Climbing out of the vehicle, she turned back to look at him watching her.

"Kindly look the other way, Sir."

Haaken turned his face away to look out of his window, with a mischievous grin lighting up his face.

A little while later with a happy sigh, Layla clambered back into the Bronco. They heard the dog grunt contentedly behind them as he slept on.

"Haaken, I've been thinking and wondering how you know about your father's secret mine?"

Still watching the road ahead, he spoke.

"Henry told me in a strange, roundabout way. I'm still trying to figure out what his angle is in all of this."

"Good question" she said nodding "There seems to have been some bad blood between your Father and old Henry."

Haaken drove on down the highway with a look of determination etching itself into his face once again as he quietly spoke.

"Indeed there was and somehow my brother has been caught up in the middle of it all."

Sensing that he needed to think, Layla settled down to sleep.

CHAPTER TWENTY THREE

The Hunter Homestead

The crunch of wheels on dirt along with the rough bouncing over an uneven road surface slowly knocked Ulfred awake. The awful banging of his head against the floor forced him to raise his head and open his eyes. Looking up through the windows at the passing trees in the early morning light made him realize they were on the road up to their family home. Ulfred quietly winced in pain from his wounds as he began to think a little more clearly about what he could possibly do to drag this out and still stay alive.

Thinking back to the ravine where he had scratched the incomplete map reference onto the door pillar jogged his memory. He remembered an old map their father had always kept rolled up on top of the old wooden kitchen dresser.

The bumpy journey up to the cabin seemed to take forever as his aching body absorbed each bump and dip in the road. Eventually the vehicle came to a stop affording Ulfred a brief moment of rest.

He could hear Ozil complaining that he could hardly keep his eyes open he was so tired. This was followed by a sharp slap and yelp, then quick footsteps around to the back of the vehicle. The rear tailgate and upper door were wrenched open and her hand reached in. She grabbed the blanket wrapped around him and roughly hauled him from the vehicle. Ulfred almost fell, but to his surprise, she easily held him up. He realized then that Morana was unusually strong. She leaned forward and spoke pleasantly into his ear.

"Come along, Ulfred. You are going to show me where this mine is, aren't you?"

Ulfred simply nodded his head in agreement as she propelled him forward with her hand on his back forcing him to hop or fall face down onto the hard cold ground. His wobbly hopping was painful in the extreme as his bare feet landed on the cold ground after each difficult hop and his feet began to go numb. As he warily battled his way to the cabin porch, the rope securing his ankles together started to work loose and he was able to shuffle forward for short distances. Still, he had to hop up the porch stairs. Reaching the porch floor, his face scrunched up with the pain, he did an awkward shuffling wriggle across it. Ulfred stood still in front of the door until Morana reached around him to open it. He slowly shuffled forward into the cabin, closely followed by Morana and the exhausted Ozil. Prodding him painfully in the back of his neck, Morana leaned close to Ulfred's ear to whisper in a quiet sultry voice laced with venom.

"Well, Ulfred" she said "I need answers now! Or perhaps you would like me to encourage you a little?"

Her tongue flicked out to lightly lick his ear, her voice now deeper with lust rising to the surface rapidly.

"A little more pain my poor baby?"

Ulfred hunched his shoulders, leaning forward to get away from her as he shuffled forward like a penguin to the kitchen and motioned to the top of the old kitchen dresser with his chin. He sank gratefully onto a kitchen chair.

Morana quickly spun one of the other chairs around and climbed onto it to retrieve the dusty rolled up map from the top of the dresser. Jumping from the chair, she quickly unrolled the map on top of the kitchen table. She secured the map's corners down on the table with a ketchup bottle, an ashtray, and a wooden butter dish.

With a savage glint in her beautiful green eyes and flared nostrils, Morana looked at Ulfred with a hint of lust beginning to show in her eyes. In a throaty tone, she spoke.

"Are you going to show me, or do I have to play with you a little more to encourage your memory?"

Barely able to lift his head, Ulfred stared at her beautiful face. *I have to convince her I know where it is or she might just start cutting bits off me again. Haaken. My brother. Where are you?*

"Ozil!" she shrieked "Untie his hands!"

Ozil, still weary and bone-tired from lack of sleep heaved himself over to Ulfred and began to remove the bindings from his hands and feet.

With a supreme effort of sheer willpower, Ulfred spoke in a voice far more confident than he was feeling.

"Give me a minute or two to check the map."

CHAPTER TWENTY FOUR

Closing In.

About two hours after sunrise, Haaken and Layla arrived in the lonely town of Solitude and stopped outside Georgio's country store.

After gently waking Layla, Haaken climbed stiffly from the truck. Stretching his legs for a few moments, he turned to pull the back of his seat forward to let the dog out. The large Rottweiler gratefully leapt from the seat to the ground and immediately turned to cock his leg on the hot rear tire of the vehicle with an obvious look of relief on his face.

"Does that feel better boy?"

The dog's stumpy tail wagged a few times as he looked up at him. Haaken stepped up onto the store porch followed by the dog and Layla. They entered the store with the jingle of the doorbell announcing their arrival. Georgio looked up from where he was busy cleaning his shop countertop. Recognizing Haaken immediately, he waved with a smile,

"Haaken how are you? How did your trip go?" he called out.

Before Haaken could reply, Georgio spotted Layla walking into the store behind him. He waved and called out a greeting.

"Good Morning Ma'am."

His eyes widened in fear when he saw the large Rottweiler step forward in front of Haaken, its top lip beginning to curl up with a growl rumbling from its barrel chest.

"Easy boy," commanded Haaken.

Immediately, the dog backed up to his side to stand patiently but alert while watching Georgio.

"Morning my old friend" said Haaken "Have you got some fresh coffee and perhaps an old map showing the area around my homestead," asked Haaken.

"Fresh coffee at the end of the counter and I'll be right back with some maps," replied Georgio as he disappeared into the back room.

He soon returned with several old maps and spread them out on the countertop. Over a large hot cup of coffee, Haaken and Layla studied them on the counter. Haaken spotted an older topographical map of the area laying further along the countertop. He scanned it, running his finger over an area to the northwest of the homestead. His finger came to rest on a spot showing an elevated rocky section with an old dry river bed dropping from the heights down to a lower elevation before disappearing.

"Where did you get this map, Georgio?" he asked.

"Years ago an old-timer came in selling his prospecting gear. This was part of it," he answered.

"Do you mind if I borrow it?"

"No problem, Haaken."

"Thank you my friend."

Turning to Layla with the map in hand, Haaken spoke.

"Let's go..." he said.

Back in the truck with the dog, Layla turned to Haaken,

"What did you see on that map?"

"Using the partial coordinates, there is a place high up to the North West of my cabin. The mine *must* be in that area. I also spotted what could be an ancient trail going up there from a point off the main road through an old river course."

As they drove out of town Haaken's mind spun in deep thought. *They must have got to the cabin by now. Do we go up to the cabin? Or do we strike out along the old river line up to the site?*

CHAPTER TWENTY FIVE

Battery.

With an unsteady hand, Ulfred traced one finger slowly over an area North West of where they were. He could feel Morana's impatience like hot waves of mounting rage washing over him as he stared down at the map. *Dear God, I pray Haaken catches up soon.* He looked up into Morana's eyes. *Oh, such beautiful eyes.* He caught his thoughts before his mind started to drown in them. *Ulfred! Get it together!* He tapped the map with his finger,

"It's close to here," he said as confidently as he could while still looking into her eyes. Her face lit up with greed and lustful excitement.

"We must go now!"

Her low sultry voice was rich with arousal and he found himself trapped like a mouse in her intense gaze with his mind beginning to unravel.

"I need boots for my feet and some clothes" he said.

She seemed to glide smoothly as a serpent from her end of the table to where he sat and suddenly and brutally smashed his nose with a clenched fist. Ulfred fell sideways from the chair, the blanket flying from his body. He immediately tried to clutch at his broken nose with his mutilated hand but failed miserably as his naked body hit the floor with a thud.

While tears streamed down his face, Ulfred looked up through dazed eyes blinking rapidly from the pain.

Bright red blood trickled from his smashed nose over his lips and down his chin to slowly begin dripping onto the floor. Morana leaned in close to his face and whispered in an ugly yet fully aroused voice.

"Oh my poor baby, I hope you aren't lying to me."

With a toss of her shiny auburn hair she yelled at Ozil to find some clothes and boots for Ulfred. Ozil, his eyes wide with fear, hurriedly went in search of some footwear and clothing. He returned with a pair of rubber boots, a large fur-lined jacket and a pair of trousers. He bent to the task of helping Ulfred dress.

Morana watched silently but impatiently as Ulfred struggled to dress his shivering naked body. The bloody mutilated hand caused him to screw up his face in pain as he pulled up the trousers. Ozil helped with the jacket and boots, before stepping away from him.

Breathing heavily, Ulfred eased himself to his feet, wiping some of the blood from his face with the jacket sleeve.

"Ok Ulfred, which way do we go?" demanded Morana, as she roughly bound his hands tightly together behind his back.

"We can follow the track in the vehicle from here for quite a long way up before it ends. From there we will have to walk and climb higher up the mountain,"

"You poor lamb, it will soon be over. Just get us to the mine!" she purred with a coy smile.

Her hard eyes glittered with a kind of manic fervour as she quickly rolled up the dusty old map. With a strong grip on Ulfred's arm, Morana propelled him out of the cabin back to their vehicle before shoving him onto the back seat. She clambered into the front passenger side while Ozil eased himself onto the driving seat.

They drove slowly away from the cabin in low gear, along the old timber road through the forest and up towards the mountain.

Ulfred stared out at the forest which was almost hidden with a white mist shrouding everything with an air of foreboding. The whole scene added to his painful unease as he sat hunched on the rear seat still trying to figure out how he could play this out for as long as possible. Maybe, just maybe, he might find an opportunity to escape. *Haaken where are you? I don't know how much longer I can keep this up!* Ulfred now in deep shock and exhausted beyond belief continued to stare at the ghostly trees shrouded in white. Slowly but surely, a deep sense of foreboding began to wrap it itself around his innermost being.

CHAPTER TWENTY SIX

Head For The Hills.

Tossing the stub of another Cohiba from the window as he drove, Haaken came to the conclusion that he would attempt to take the river line up to the Double H mine.

Glancing over at Layla, he spoke.

"I'm sure by now they will have moved on from the cabin in their search for the mine. I think it would be pointless to try and catch them at the cabin. We must take a more direct route to get to the mine before they do. Judging from the map, I'm sure we can get off the road about twenty minutes before the turn off up to the homestead,"

Layla quietly agreed with his reasoning as she watched the road ahead of the speeding Bronco and the frozen countryside flashing by. *It'll be damned cold up there!*

After another hour of driving, Haaken slowed down to a crawl keeping an eye on the scrub to his right.

"There!" he suddenly exclaimed, pointing to a dry and rocky river bed.

Carefully pulling off the road, he engaged four-wheel drive.

Looking at Layla, he spoke with a touch of excitement creeping into his voice,

"Shall we?"

Even the dog sensed the moment and pushed its broad head between the front seats to see.

Driving slowly down off the main road into the old river bed, Haaken proceeded to cautiously drive along through the rough terrain. After fifteen minutes they noticed what could only be an ancient, almost invisible track leading up out of the old river course to their left.

Haaken stopped the truck and walked over to check it out, closely followed by Layla and the dog which now faithfully followed him wherever he went. Walking slowly back and forth he inspected the old track for signs of usage. Then ahead he spied an old mud dried wheel track.

"This track has definitely been used by a vehicle before." he said.

Even the dog confirmed this by sniffing the old tire track.

Returning to the truck, Haaken opened the neatly folded old map from Georgio and laid it out on the seat. It showed the local area they were in and the mountainous area beyond where he suspected the mine might be.

"Let's drive along the track for a while and see if it follows the old river line up into the mountains. If it does, we should be able to make better time getting up there."

They drove up onto the track, which sure enough, followed the old river line. However, they were only able to keep moving at a speed a little faster than a crawl.

"Looks like it could take another hour or so to get up there, assuming that the track goes all the way. If it doesn't, we'll have a tough climb ahead", he commented.

With a deeply worried look on her face, Layla spoke.

"I hope this old track goes further than we think."

It was fifteen minutes later before anyone spoke.

"You had better just check over my rifle" said Haaken "There's a spare box of bullets on the storage shelf by your knees. We need to start keeping a sharp eye out for any movement up ahead of us."

Layla immediately got busy with the rifle.

CHAPTER TWENTY SEVEN

Onwards & Upwards.

༄

The black SUV struggled on up the old timber track, slipping and sliding on the wet icy ground. The vehicle had no four-wheel drive ability, only diff-lock to help the back wheels improve their traction on the treacherous terrain.

After just twenty minutes of climbing, the vehicle slithered to a halt, it's back wheels spinning uselessly.

"You fucking idiot!" shrieked Morana "Look what you've gone and done! You got the damned car stuck!"

She turned to Ozil and slammed her fist into the side of his head in a frenzy of maniacal madness. His head hit the door window and bounced back into an upright position. Slumping forward, semi-conscious, he struck the car horn with his forehead. The instant, deafening blaring of the vehicle horn echoed and bounced around the mountainside until Morana grabbed Ozil by the hair and yanked his head back to the seat headrest to halt the noise.

"Idiot!"She shrieked into his ear again.

Clumsily, the still dazed Ozil managed to reverse the vehicle but in doing so he gunned the engine causing the back end to snake sideways. He then overcorrected the steering as the spinning back wheels found purchase on some exposed tree roots and small stones. This unfortuate action propelled the SUV forward like a rock from a slingshot.

Ozil stared ahead through the windshield in dumb fascination as the large fir tree loomed out of the light mist. The SUV, with engine roaring, rammed it head-on like an enraged bull. All that could be heard after the vehicle slammed into the tree was the slow ticking of the hot exhaust under the mangled hood along with a strange bubbly rasping sound.

Ulfred had been slammed forward into the back of the front passenger seat at the moment of impact. Painfully easing himself up and back onto the back seat, he took in the disturbing image of Ozil.

Head and face covered in white powder from the burst airbag, Ozil's wide eyes stared up at the roof. His neck had been impaled on a jagged branch from the tree that had come through the windscreen and was nailed to the headrest. The strange, bubbly, rasping sound was coming from Ozil's severed windpipe as bright frothy blood pumped copiously from his mangled neck.

A high pitched scream of rage from Morana brought Ulfred out of his shocked daze. Turning to look at her, he jerked his head back in fright at the sight of her ghostly white face with blood running from her nose. *The dashboard airbag has certainly done a number on your face as well!* Morana stared at the grim scene in silence. Then, almost mechanically, she reached over and turned off the ignition key, cutting off the red ignition light which had lit up the macabre scene with a pale red glow.

Before Ulfred could think of trying to escape, Morana opened her door, almost falling down as she climbed out onto the slippery track. She yanked open his door and hauled him out of the vehicle with a vice-like grip around his bound wrists. *She's unbelievable!* Ulfred's mind screamed silently as he fell to the muddy track.

"Get up you fucking imbecile!" She shouted down into his face.

Her features contorted into a ghostly white powdered blood-streaked mask from hell. Ulfred rolled painfully onto his knees and managed to stand up without any further encouragement.

"What about Ozil?" he asked quietly.

Morana glared at him then turned to look through the open door of the vehicle.

"The lazy piece of shit is dead!" she said with a sneer.

Morana spat on the ground and quickly turned her anger on Ulfred with a swift kick to his battered groin. He fell writhing to the ground, gasping for air. She reached into the vehicle for a bottle of water and liberally splashed her face, wiping it dry with her warm woollen scarf. She looked down at Ulfred with a bright smile made more macabre from the streaks of white powder and blood smeared across her cheeks.

"Ulfred, my dear" she said "You had better get up. We must move on."

He could hardly believe his ears, but valiantly complied and struggled to his feet in case she suddenly lashed out and kicked him again.

He watched as she retrieved a pistol from the glove box and snatched up the map, then without looking back at the vehicle, she pushed him on up the steepening track.

CHAPTER TWENTY EIGHT

The Double H Mine.

Haaken's Bronco laboured along slowly as it ground its way along the worn track which had faithfully followed the winding, rock-strewn river course ever higher. His truck managed without getting stuck as they crept towards the steeper slopes of the mountain ahead. They stopped briefly to stretch their legs and check the map once again to gauge their progress.

"I have a feeling this track doesn't go much further..." said Haaken "From then we will be on foot."

He stood silently for a few minutes listening to the wilderness surrounding them and taking note of the mist creeping down from the higher ground.

"Let's move on..."

Suddenly Haaken froze. Even the dog stopped sniffing around and stood still with its head held high. They stared up at the high ground above them. The sound of a car horn in the distance broke the silence for several seconds before stopping abruptly. Layla looked across at Haaken.

"That must be them." he muttered darkly.

They climbed back into the warm cab of the Bronco and slowly drove on up the ever-increasing gradient of the track. After another twenty minutes the track came to an end in a small open area where a vehicle could turn around to head back down the track.

"Looks like we walk from here," said Haaken.

He let the dog out from the back seat and shouldered his backpack. With her own backpack slung over one shoulder, Layla passed him the rifle and they proceeded up an old pathway that appeared to have been well used in the past. In total silence, they made their way up the path following the old watercourse passing great piles of loose rock. They carefully climbed higher and higher up the steep, slippery slope until finally they crested a ridge. There they found themselves standing on a small plateau with large rocks and boulders on either side.

Across the small plateau, Haaken spotted the entrance to an old mine working. The dark opening dug into the mountainside was near where the old watercourse seemed to rise from the base of the mountain above. Crouching down, Haaken cautioned Layla to do the same and motioned the dog to his side. He carefully scanned the entire area for a good five minutes until he was satisfied there was no movement in the vicinity.

"Okay..." he said quietly "Let's go and see what we have here, but keep your eyes and ears peeled for anything."

Layla nodded without saying a word and quietly followed Haaken and the dog slowly across the small open area to the rough blasted opening in the rock face. When they arrived at the entrance Haaken could see that the rough blasted rock opening disappeared into the mountainside. He observed a steady stream of icy water running out from the dark tunnel and across the open plateau. Dropping his pack, he rummaged inside it and produced a powerful torch.

"Well..." he said with a tight smile "Looks like we had better take a look inside the Double H Mine and see what my Father was up to,"

Haaken had never enjoyed going underground. The absolute darkness, where no light existed, had always felt like a heavy mantle of dark power. A power always ready to snuff out a life like a hapless candle in the wind.

"I don't like going under the ground..." said Layla nervously "It gives me the creeps."

Even the dog appeared to shiver nervously as it peered into the darkness of the tunnel.

"It's okay, Layla" said Haaken "I agree, I hate it too. Just follow me a short distance in. When you are out of sight you can wait for me there. You can also keep an eye out front while I check to see how deep the tunnel goes"

Bending low at the tunnel opening which was only five and a half feet high, Haaken entered slowly, shining the torch beam ahead to light the way. A few feet into the tunnel Layla stopped, dropped her pack to the ground next to Haaken's pack, and sat down on it facing the mine entrance.

Haaken handed Layla his rifle, smiled at her then turned and moved off slowly, heading deeper into the mine.

The dog looked from Layla to Haaken as he began to disappear around a small bend in the tunnel. It made up its mind with a low whine, and trotted off after Haaken.

"Well now..." muttered Layla as she stared out "Looks like it's just me and the rifle,"

Stumbling, Haaken made his way along the dark wet tunnel in an awkward half-crouch with his feet splashing in the running water. He began to see signs of serious deterioration in the rocky roof, cracked walls, and the basic timber shoring which had rotted away with the passage of time.

He struggled with the scattered rocks lying in wait on the floor for any misplaced foot. Cautiously he moved forward, wary of falling or bashing his head on the low rocky roof. He cast the torch beam from the floor to the walls and along the roof of the tunnel. This angled upwards the deeper he went and it occurred to him that this was the reason for the slow trickle of water running out of the entrance.

Haaken saw very little sign of gold. *He must have been following a small vein of gold the way this tunnel meanders first one way then another.* He thought pausing to catch his breath. The going was hard inn his half crouched position. The dog sat down, tongue lolling from his mouth looking at Haaken expectantly. He reached back to pat him on the head,

"We had better see what's around this next corner, boy."

Haaken scrambled forward with difficulty as the rocky roof became even lower at this point. He was eventually forced to come down onto his hands and knees. Haaken continued to crawl forward, the torch beam bouncing from floor to wall and ahead into the frozen darkness.

Emerging into a slightly wider area, he managed to almost stand up and saw that the tunnel roof had been blasted a lot higher at this point.

A pale glint of white appeared up ahead. Pausing to stretch his back and get into a better position, Haaken shone the torch ahead with a steady hand. Its beam sliced into the darkness revealing the white bones of the upper half of a human skeleton sticking out from a small rockfall. The lower half of the body had been pinned down by a large slab of rock.

"Holy Shit!" said Haaken loudly.

He almost dropped the torch and painfully knocked his head on the low roof as his body jerked upwards at the startling sight of the bones. The hair on the back of his neck stood up and Haaken felt that the darkness down there was reaching out to smother him. He forced himself slowly forward to the trapped body which was now only the skeletal remains of some poor soul. The pale bones told a sad story of someone trapped and unable to extricate himself from the rockfall. Someone who had met with a slow, horrible, and lonely death of starvation and utter isolation.

Carefully squatting down on the floor, he began to examine the remnants of rotted clothing. The aluminium belt buckle caught his attention and he carefully reached down to turn it over. With a sharp intake of breath the whites of his wide-open eyes glinting in the torchlight.

Haaken discovered to his horror that he was looking at his father. He recognized what was left of Dad's favourite leather belt with the bucking bronco belt buckle engraved with the words 'Harry Hunter' on the back. His thoughts spun in a terrible turmoil. *Dear Lord. What an awful way to go. All this time I thought you had deserted us... I'm so sorry for doubting you, Dad.*

Tears ran silently from Haaken's eyes as he struggled to breathe with the intense emotion evoked in his innermost being. The terrible sadness of what had happened all those years ago tore at his heart and soul. Clearing his throat, he studied the rockfall and the way it had trapped his father. The big Rottweiler inched forward on his belly to rest its head on Haaken's outstretched leg.

"Well boy" he whispered, looking around the cavern "Looks like we found the old man. And perhaps a name for you,"

He ruffled the dog's ears with a strong hand and said the word loudly and firmly to the dog.

"Rocky!"

Immediately pricking up its ears, the dog gave Haaken a lopsided doggy smile, lifted half his top lip to expose his front teeth and wagged his stumpy tail. It was then that Haaken noticed the scratch marks on one of the smoother rocks near the bones. They were barely visible in the torchlight. Leaning forward with excitement, he reached over and with a broad sweep of his hand he cleared the dust from the scratched markings to reveal words in Latin.

Once again the hair on the back of Haaken's neck rose and his body came up in goosebumps. Tense and wide-eyed, he read the few barely legible lines that his father had managed to scratch into the hard rock.

'Henrici mori hic dereliquit me' Haaken read the Latin words aloud with a grim look of anger upon his face as he translated the words.

"Henry left me here to die..."

CHAPTER TWENTY NINE

Ulfred & The Double H Mine.

Some time after abandoning their vehicle, Ulfred and Morana came to the end of the timber track and emerged onto rough, rocky terrain. She brutally pushed him on, never letting up as he staggered in constant pain over the rocks on the precarious path. Some were sharp enough to cut to the bone if one were to fall while the smaller loose ones could cause a climber to lose their footing and tumble to a hasty end. Ulfred staggered onwards, his eyes no longer seeing clearly. Slipping and sliding, they persevered on the wet rocky ground as they slowly moved up to the the higher ground above. To Ulfred it seemed like an eternity.

Suddenly he was jerked to a halt as Morana grabbed the back of his collar, pulling him viciously backwards. He slipped and fell heavily onto his back. Unable to cushion his fall with his hands still tightly tied behind him, a sharp rock sliced into his mutilated hand. Ulfred, almost at the limit of his endurance, could only gasp aloud and almost passed out. Morana raised her handgun upraised to strike him.

"Be quiet!" she hissed.

With difficulty, Ulfred held his breath, his heart beating wildly in his chest as he stared up at the raised weapon. He weakly drew his knees up to his chest in a defensive reaction.

Morana was staring intently up at the higher ground ahead of them. Then he heard it too. It was the sound of a powerful engine, followed by silence.

Morana glared down at Ulfred with a demented look of pure hatred.

"Your bastard half brother, Haaken has beaten us to the mine!"

She lashed out at one of his knees with the barrel of the gun. Ulfred winced and gasped in pain from the clubbing. Silently his inner thoughts screamed. *I hope you die soon, you fucking horrible bitch!* He lay staring fearfully up at her from the ground, half expecting another lashing.

Morana reached down and roughly hauled him to his feet, her hot breath in one ear. Nudging her nose against the back of his ear and sniffing his hair, she whispered in tense, sensual undertones,

"Make a sound, darling and I will enjoy cutting off some more bits of you!"

Meekly, Ulfred nodded his head in silence as she forced him on, ever upwards, in the direction that the engine sound had come from.

It did not take them long to reach the small open area where Haaken had parked his Bronco. *Thank God for small mercies. Haaken is here!* Thought Ulfred as a small ray of hope filtered through the remnants of his shattered mind.

Morana quickly approached the vehicle, checking in the back and then opening the driver's door to look inside.

A look of triumph lit up her blood-smeared face as she held up the ignition keys for Ulfred to see. He groaned inwardly. *Fuck! Her luck never runs out!* Morana motioned him to move up the trail towards the ridge above them. With a grunt of pure agony, Ulfred forced himself slowly upwards along the slippery trail. Nearing the ridge he lost his footing and fell heavily to the ground dislodging a few rocks which clattered down the slope. Easing himself up onto his hands and knees, he looked up in alarm as Morana rapidly stepped up to him. It was too late for him to duck the rapidly descending barrel. Morana Renwick pistol-whipped his head in a fit of pure rage. Ulfred collapsed senseless to the ground in a ragged heap.

"Quiet, you fucking moron!" She muttered through clenched teeth.

Then, kicking him again for good measure, she scrambled up to the edge of the ridge. At that point, Morana heard the sound of Layla's voice and quickly crouched down behind a large rock. Carefully peering around the ragged edge, she could see the dark, rough-cut entrance to the mine across the small flat open area ahead of her.

CHAPTER THIRTY

Double Trouble.

Inside the entrance and partially hidden from view in the dimly lit opening, Layla called out to Haaken that she was going to check on the unusual sound she had heard outside on that rapidly darkening day. A few rocks had fallen down the slope across from the entrance. Haaken was sitting down on the rough floor facing the remains of his father after reading the final chapter of his life so laboriously carved into the face of the very rocks that had crushed him. He was attempting to carefully withdraw the old leather belt and buckle by moving some large rocks around the upper skeletal remains of Harry Hunter. Suddenly he paused and looked over his shoulder in alarm as Layla's voice echoed indistinctly down the tunnel, bouncing off the rough-hewn rocky walls.

"Haak…….rocks……down far side……they…… to check." was all heard.

Shit! She's going outside. That's not a good idea! In his haste to get back to Layla he tugged desperately at the old leather belt jammed between two large rocks. Glaring at the stubborn belt in the waning light from his torch, he leaned back and put all his body weight into the pull. Suddenly the length of belt sprang free from the heavy pincer grip of the rocks, bringing with it the remnants of Harry's aged jeans along with a portion of his pelvis. Haaken fell clumsily backwards with widened eyes as the pale portion of pelvis appeared to catapult itself from the pile of rocks towards him. This was followed by a loud crack as the heavy upper rock dropped into the small space vacated by the belt. Landing heavily on his back with forearms raised to fend off the incoming portion of Harry's pelvis, Haaken managed to swat the flying bone to the side. He let out a loud gasp as the pent up air in his lungs was expelled in a rush as he landed on his back on the hard floor of the tunnel. Rocky had rapidly scrambled backward out of the way with a startled growl. Lying on his back, Haaken smiled in triumph as he raised the freed piece of old leather belt and the aluminium buckle above him. He sucked in a fresh lungful of damp, musty air as the belt buckle glinted in the reflected light of the torch. Crawling up to Haaken on his belly, Rocky licked his face with concern. Haaken smiled and scratched the dog's ears.

"I'm okay, buddy..." he said.

It was at that moment another loud crack from the pile of rocks reverberated off the tunnel walls only to be followed by a low rumble and slight tremor through the tunnel floor. Haaken looked up at the rock pile and rough unprotected roof above him in alarm while the dog whined and began to back away growling deep in his chest.

"Oh Shit!!" he said loudly.

While still lying on his back, he started to scramble backward using his hands and feet to propel him. Suddenly a group jagged splits appeared in the roof behind the rock. They spread instantaneously along the roof over Haaken's head like a thunderbolt and disappeared into the sidewall. This was backed up by a heavier tremor that shook the whole chamber.

Immediately after the main ground shaking tremor, several more light tremors followed, causing several very large rocks and a multitude of smaller ones to break out from the roof and fall to the tunnel floor in a violent crescendo of thunderous power. The entire scene appeared to be moving in slow motion as Haaken stared in wide-eyed horror at the jagged cracks and falling rocks. His body felt like it was stuck in treacle as he attempted to clear his legs out of the way. But it was too late. The jumble of tumbling jagged rocks landed on his leg followed by yet another jagged piece of the rock wall which broke free and crashed down on one side of his chest. Haaken yelled in fright and shock, his hands desperately trying to pull himself out of the way. He let out another very loud yell of intense pain as he felt a couple of his ribs crack. This was followed quickly by a bolt of pain that shot up his right leg that was now pinned down by the heavy rocks that had been dislodged from the same pile that covered the skeleton.

An eerie silence descended upon the dusty scene. The only sound was that of his coughing and spluttering. He spat out bits of stray dirt and rock matter along with the fine, choking dust that threatened to asphyxiate him. With eyes now streaming with tears, he blinked rapidly to try and clear the irritating dust and gritty particles that had enveloped him.

CHAPTER THIRTY ONE

Layla

After shouting back down the tunnel to Haaken, Layla cautiously moved from the safety of the mine entrance out onto the open area beyond. With rifle raised, she nervously swung the barrel in an arc from left to right and back. All was quiet. Far too quiet. Layla walked slowly forward toward the large rock on the edge of the clearing where the trail they had climbed emerged onto the small plateau. Still listening intently and rapidly shifting her eyes from the trees, to rocks and shadows, she tried desperatelyto see if anyone was there.

Layla was peering intently down the slope, looking along the side of the large rock and down the trail when she heard the rumble and felt the slight tremor through her feet. Spinning around to look back at the mine entrance, she saw a thick cloud of dust forcibly expelled from its mouth like the exhalation of an angry dragon. Layla's right hand flew to her mouth as she gazed in terror, realizing that something truly terrible had happened.

"Oh Lord. No!" She screamed as she started to run back to the entrance.

Taking advantage of Layla's distress, Morana rose swiftly from where she lay hidden. Like a lion springing forward to make a kill, she cut rapidly across the open space between them to neatly trip her up. Layla flew headlong and face down into the stony ground. The rifle flew from her grip while she desperately tried to break her fall with her hands. She slid painfully along the rough ground before coming to an abrupt stop, wincing in pain at her cut and bruised palms.

"Hello Layla," purred Morana.

Morana drove a firm booted foot down into the middle of Layla's back, pinning her to the ground.

Layla groaned in pain as her breath was brutally driven from her lungs. She desperately twisted her head around to look up at Morana, and spat out in a rasping gasp

"You bitch!"

Morana smiled pleasantly while applying even more pressure to Layla's lower back, forcing another groan of agony from her.

CHAPTER THIRTY TWO

Trapped!

Haaken struggled for air in the heavy choking dust which had blocked his eyes, his nostrils, and coated his tongue and throat with fine dust particles. Working up as much saliva as he could with his tongue, he spat a muddy globule of spit at the floor as he hawked his throat to try and clear it.

His dust impregnated eyes were almost glued closed from the muddy mix of tears and fine dust. Haaken tried to wipe the fine-grained mess from his eyes while realizing he was now trapped in the tight confines of the tunnel in total darkness.

His shocked mind began to register the reason he could actually see was because of a minor stroke of luck. His torch had miraculously rolled undamaged into a small shallow divot in the floor where it lay pointing a weak beam upwards through the settling dust. It was a consolation that he could see instead of being trapped in total darkness. *A small plus! I fucking hate the confines of this dark place. Now, how the hell am I going to get myself out of this mess?* Laughing nervously and wincing from his broken ribs, he muttered aloud.

"Damn, almost finished up like Dad. Rocky! Hey boy!" he called out to the dog.

His fear was that it was seriously hurt or worse from the rockfall. With relief he saw the big dog, completely covered in fine dust, crawling nervously out of the dusty gloom towards him to lick his face. Haaken sighed with relief.

"You're okay buddy…" He said patting the dog.

There was some comfort in their new companionship. As the dust settled, Haaken pushed himself up into a sitting position to check the damage to his legs from the falling rocks. Reaching for the torch, he could see the rocks trapping his right leg. As he played the torch beam over the walls and roof above him, he noticed some sharp yellow gleams near the top of the pile of fallen rock. The narrow band of quartz clearly showing gold particles could now be clearly seen. They were embedded in the newly exposed tunnel roof. He stared up at it in amazement. *Wow. That has to be the gold seam Dad was chasing when the roof came down on him!*

As if to remind him how precarious his position was, there was a low rumble and slight settling of the rock pile. It was as though the ancient mountain was challenging him, hinting at the difficulty and danger in extracting the precious metal from its rocky grip. Cringing in anticipation of more violent wrath from the cracked rock around him, Haaken immediately focused on getting himself out of this dire predicament.

With a painful grunt, he managed to lean forward to push the first heavy rock from his leg. His broken ribs ached deeply from the effort.

Eventually he managed to carefully heave the rock off his leg. It tumbled over to land with a loud thud against the huge pile that towered above him. *Shit!* He looked up with apprehension as his body tensed in anticipation of more rocks tumbling from the pile in front of him.

Heaving a painful sigh of relief when nothing happened, his mind wandered back to Layla. He thoughts were desperate. *I've got to get back to the tunnel entrance. Layla must be in trouble. I've heard nothing from her since she went outside to check on whatever she felt needed checking on. Damn it! That mad, psychotic Morana could be lurking out there close by! Layla could be in some serious trouble!*

Positioning the torch on some loose rocks, Haaken could now see that the piece of jagged rock canted over at an angle against the wall had neatly trapped his shin and foot in the small gap. No matter how he tried to wriggle his foot, it would not come free. *Shit! Shit! Shit! Calm down buddy, and think!*

Reaching as far forward as his damaged ribs would allow, he pushing a little further to get his hands on the rock. Haaken tried in vain to move in an effort to extricate his foot. It was to no avail. Sweating profusely from the effort, he lay back on the wet muddy floor in utter frustration and let out a deep gut grunt of pain. The dog crawled forward to sniff his face with concern.

"I'm okay, Rocky.." he panted "Just really pissed off! I need a lever of some kind."

Checking his lower body for his trusty tomahawk, Haaken realised the damn thing had somehow come loose when he had fallen and was no longer there. *What now?* he thought desperately as he lay back again and stared up at the thin seam of gold above. The glint of it seemed to mock him as he lay there near the remains of his father. He shifted slightly on the wet rocky floor to ease the uncomfortable length of the large Bowie knife digging into his back. This sparked an idea. *Haaken Hunter! You are a dumb asshole! Use the knife to lever the rock away!*

Rolling a little to one side, he reached back over his shoulder to draw the knife. The sharp stabbing pain from his ribs stopped him in mid-reach. *Damn that hurt!* Rolling partially onto the other side, he unbuckled the leather straps holding the knife and let it fall to the ground beneath his partially raised back. With a wince and some effort, he pulled the whole ensemble around onto his stomach.

Carefully drawing the large heavy-duty ten inch blade from its leather sheath, Haaken once again leaned forward and with the extra reach of the blade managed to wedge it a good few inches between the wall and the large jagged piece of broken rock. He began to use the blade as a lever to ease the rock away from the sidewall. More beads of sweat popped up on his face and neck from the strain. Hearing a slight crunching noise as the heavy rock moved away from the wall he eased his foot out from where it lay trapped between the two and found to his relief that it moved more freely. But his arms now began to shake from the strain of holding the rock away from the wall. Closing his eyes and levering harder with the blade, he managed to move it a little more. As he pulled and twisted, his foot suddenly came free from the tight space. At the same time, the few inches of blade wedged between the rock and the wall snapped with a loud crack. Haaken quickly rolled backward to put some distance between himself and the rock pile as it crashed back against the wall.

Panting heavily from the effort and still gripping the Bowie knife handle, he grunted from the sharp stabbing pain in his ribs. Warily Haaken eyed the rock pile and tunnel roof. *Dear God, I hope noth-*

ing else comes crashing down! Absolute silence greeted him in the gloomy half-light of the torch beam scattered with dust motes.

He rolled up the torn piece of his father's leather belt and buckle and pocketed it. Haaken shoved the broken bowie knife back into its sheath and carefully strapped the ensemble back on. Taking a moment to search the area, he found his tomahawk where it had spun away as it was torn from its leather loop during the rockfall. It lay trapped nearby under a few smaller rocks. Carefully retrieving it, he turned around on his hands and knees and began making his way out of the tunnel as quickly as he could with Rocky closely following on his heels.

CHAPTER THIRTY THREE

Morana & Haaken.

Staring down at Layla squirming under her boot face down in the dirt, Morana laughed out loud as she pressed her victim harder into the rocky ground. She ground her heel against Layla's spine. Sweating and gritting her teeth against the pain in her back, Layla desperately tried to wriggle free, all the while frantic with worry about Haaken who she believed to be trapped in the mine. *He might be badly hurt, or worse!* With a supreme effort of iron will and desperate determination, Layla managed to lift herself and roll free from Morana's boot. At the same time, she reached out to grab the offending leg to upend her attacker.

Morana fell heavily to the ground onto her back, with a loud

'Oomph!'

Instantly she rolled, cat-like onto her stomach and sprung upright in time to launch a brutal kick to Layla's head as she rose from the ground. Layla's torn, bloody hands could not fend off the incoming kick and her head snapped back from the blow as she dropped to her knees in a daze. Down on all fours, Layla spat blood from her mouth as she tried to focus her blurry eyes on Morana. The painful thud of a knee in her back together with a powerful hand gripping her by the hair forcing her head back, told her where Morana stood. Layla's eyes focused on Morana's hate-filled, snarling face above her.

"Trying to hurt me? You soft bitch!" spat Morana with droplets of spittle flying into Layla's face.

Viciously yanking Layla's head further backward, she drove a bony knee savagely into her back causing her to moan in agony.

Morana began to pant, her sensuous voice low, as she leaned down towards Layla's contorted face and whispered into her ear.

"You poor girl, does it hurt? Yes! It does you poor baby, it hurts so badly!"

Savagely, Morana chopped down on Layla's face with her pistol butt, instantly smashing her nose. She followed up by pounding the pistol butt into her temple as she let her hair go. Layla slumped unconscious to the ground with bubbles of blood expelling from her nose every time she breathed.

Standing up with a satisfied smile and stretching as she moved her head from side to side to ease her neck, Morana kicked Layla as hard as she could in the stomach. Then she turned away and walked across to the mine entrance.

With a look of pure malice on her twisted face, her mind reaching out with absolute hatred, she screamed into the dark mine.

"Haaken Hunter!! Now you belong to me!"

Like a silent heavy black meteorite plunging from space, Rocky's massive body burst from the mine entrance and flew at speed across the small plateau. The dog collided head on with Morana, his large solid head hit her like a battering ram and knocked Morana flying towards the edge of the plateau. This was closely followed by Haaken's yell as he limped across the open space towards them, favouring his damaged ribs.

"Rocky!" he cried out.

Immediately the big dog stopped where he was. Standing still he stared at Morana with heavy lips lifted to expose his large canines in a menacing snarl.

Morana screamed like a psychotic banshee incensed with blind rage as she scrambled to her feet. She wobbled unsteadily on the loose rocky edge of the plateau and screamed again with frothy spittle spraying from her beautiful full lips.

"Haaken Hunter! Your bastard Father's gold is mine and mine alone!"

Morana still held her pistol which she now levelled at Haaken's head. He dived sideways, hitting the ground with his shoulder and painfully compressing his damaged ribs as he rolled over. He came up in a crouch, his face grimacing in pain.

He expected to hear the pistol fire or take a hit, but there was nothing but silence. He saw that Rocky was now leaning slightly forward, head cocked over at an odd angle as he listened intently with both ears.

What the fuck?! Thought Haaken, staring at an empty space where Morana had been standing. *She's disappeared! How?*

The only sound was the clatter of loose rocks tumbling down the slope away from the edge of the plateau. Then there was a moan from Layla who lay nearby, still face down on the rocks.

CHAPTER THIRTY FOU

Morana Runs.

As she squeezed the trigger, the crumbly plateau edge gave way dropping Morana like a stone down the steep scree slope. Scrabbling desperately with her hands to try to slow her momentum, she slid over the sharp rocks on her stomach only coming to rest next to Ulfred's semi-conscious body.

With a crazed look of pure insanity she jumped to her feet quite oblivious to the cuts, scrapes, and bruising from her rapid descent. Her eyes darted frantically about stopping only when she saw the pistol which had slid and bounced to land nearby. Her face twisted into a lopsided smile as she leapt forward to retrieve it.

Returning to Ulfred, she crouched down by his side and stroked his forehead, her eyes narrowing with evil intent as she calmly stared down at his face. Despite her outer calm, Morana's mind swirled in a seething turmoil of evil thoughts and intentions. *It's mine, only mine! They want to take it from me! No! No! No! no! I will not allow them to take my gold. They must die!*

With a twitch of her head, Morana focused on Ulfred whose eyes had begun to open. With a dazed look of incomprehension he looked up at her. Still stroking his forehead, she crooned lightly.

"Hush my poor baby, it will soon be over."

Through the fog of his battered mind, Ulfred instinctively knew he was in dire straits, but he still could not help himself. *She still looks so beautiful. Even with all the bruises and cuts.* His mind instantly balked at the thought, making him flinch away from her as his body reminded him of the pain he had endured so recently. Morana seized Ulfred by his jaw, forcing his mouth open to roughly insert the barrel of the pistol into his mouth. Ulfred, his eyes now alert with fear, could not hold back the hoarse moan which escaped from his dry throat. Glaring at him, Morana threw her head back and shrieked out at the top of her voice,

"I will kill you all! The gold is mine, and only mine!"

Her voice echoed around the rocky mountain. Her cunning mind knew no bounds as she plotted their end. *I must get away and plan their slow death. The gold is mine! They can't have it! I will return to collect it!*

Morana brutally pulled the barrel of her pistol from Ulfred's mouth, knocking out a front tooth and cutting his top lip in the process. As she sprang to her feet Ulfred yelled in pain and fright. Morana Renwick turned and screamed up the steep slope,

"Haaken Hunter! Your brother is mine to keep!"

Calmly, she looked down at Ulfred who was now shaking violently from fear and cold. When he opened his mouth to plead with her, she simply pointed the pistol at him. Before he could utter a sound, the pulsing bang of the pistol shot rang out loudly.

Morana spun around to sprint away, her laughter echoing through the trees and off the mountainside like the deranged cackle of some mad witch.

CHAPTER THIRTY FIVE

Haaken & Ulfred

Turning sharply at the sound of Layla's groan, Haaken rushed to her side. Getting down on his knees, he gently turned Layla over and eased her into a sitting position.

Aghast at the damage to her face, he called out,

"Layla, Layla! Can you hear me?"

Nodding her head slowly, she spoke through bruised lips and a blocked, broken nose,

"I'm okay, where is that bitch, Morana?"

As if she had heard Layla, Moranas shrieks carried clearly up to them on the plateau. They both looked up, startled at the volume.

"I have to get my brother from her," said Haaken desperately.

"Go, Haaken, and hurry!" she replied.

Haaken got to his feet and gently took her hand, placing it on Rocky's neck.

"Stay with the dog." he said.

He set off at a rapid sprint across the plateau towards the trail, trying to ignore his ribs. He had only taken four steps, when he clearly heard Morana's voice rise up again screaming like a banshee.

"Haaken Hunter! Your brother is mine to keep!"

Immediately the sound of her pistol rent the air. The percussive airwave reverberated in his ears followed by the insane cackle of Morana's laughter. Haaken, now truly feared for his brother's life. The stabbing pain of his ribs forgotten, he plunged down the steep rocky slope, slipping and sloming his way down to where Ulfred lay motionless. His mind silently screamed. *She killed him, Oh Dear Lord please, don't let Ulfred die!* Sliding to a wobbly halt next to Ulfred, Haaken sank down on his knees to gently lift his brother's head.

"Ulfred, Ulfred! Talk to me buddy!"

Ulfred opened his eyes to stare with obvious relief up at his brother and whispered in a weak voice.

"Haaken, help me my brother," he whispered before losing consciousness.

When Haaken checked over Ulfred's slack body, his hands came away, sticky with blood. Thinking Morana had shot him in the stomach, Haaken's mind reeled in shock. *No, no, no! Not a gut shot!* Carefully pulling away his bloody jacket and shirt to expose the ugly wound, Haaken let out a small sigh of nervous relief. In her haste, Morana's shot had missed his stomach and gone through the fleshy side of Ulfred's hip, leaving an ugly bloody groove as it passed on into the ground.

"Hang in there, Ulfred. You will live. Now, all we have to do is get you home..."

Ulfred, now conscious again, smiled weakly as he clutched Haaken's hands, the only real anchor in his life.

Haaken smiled happily down at his brother.

"What have you gotten yourself into bro?"

CHAPTER THIRTY SIX

Homeward Bound.

Holding Ulfred's head up, Haaken stared bleakly down the mountain in the direction Morana had bolted. *You will pay dearly for this you horrible waste of a human being.* Several small rocks skittered passed as Layla and Rocky scrambled down to where he sat by his brother's side.

"Oh my Lord, is he okay?" Gasped Layla in a nasal voice, her nose caked in dry blood.

"He is still alive, but he's going into serious shock. We have got to get him down to the truck as soon as possible!" replied Haaken.

A small tug on his hand from Ulfred got his full attention. He leaned down to listen as Ulfred spoke weakly but clearly.

"She has got your keys."

"Shit!, fucking hell!" yelled Haaken.

Realising that Morana intended to escape with his vehicle, Haaken quietly cursed himself again for leaving the keys in the ignition. *You dumb assed idiot!*

Quickly working out a plan, Haaken turned to Layla,

"Please take over here and watch Ulfred. I must get our backpacks and make up a wooden frame to drag Ulfred back home with us."

Layla immediately sat down to rest Ulfred's head on her lap as Haaken wearily clambered to his feet,

"I will be as quick as I can." he said.

Looking up the steep slope, Haaken shook his head and moved upwards with Rocky close on his heels. Cresting the top, he strode quickly across the small plateau to the mine entrance. Shouldering his pack and picking up Layla's, Haaken stared for a moment into the dark tunnel. *I will return for you, Dad.*

Abruptly turning away, he headed back across the plateau and eased himself down the slippery slope to where Layla rested with Ulfred. Retrieving a bottle of water from one of the packs, Haaken knelt at Ulfred's side,

"Here, drink some water, brother."

Ulfred gratefully sucked from the bottle to ease his parched throat and quench his thirst. Pulling back from the bottle, he started to struggle up into a sitting position, only to collapse back down, his energy spent,

"Thanks Haaken, I needed that."

"Easy bro, stay down. I will make a hand travois to haul you out of here, but first we need to get you down to the lower ground. Then I can drag you to where the timber track ends. It'll be easier than trying to cross higher up."

Between them, they managed to get Ulfred onto his feet.

Setting off down the slope, with Ulfred hanging onto their shoulders, they eventually got to the flat ground where Haaken's vehicle had been parked; now just an empty space.

Setting Ulfred down with Layla, Haaken immediately set off across the open area towards some young saplings. With his razor-sharp tomahawk, he proceeded to hack down two long saplings and several shorter ones. Laying the two longer saplings on the ground, he crossed the upper third over each other to form two handles. Then taking several shorter lengths he laid them across the longer sections, to form a rough ladder with the widest rung near the bottom.

Having retrieved a roll of nylon cord from his backpack, Haaken proceeded to bind the limbs together. *Good thing I keep that cord in the pack.* He took several thinner and more supple lengths of saplings and wove them in between the cross members to close the wide gaps and form a supporting lattice for the bed. Grabbing a pile of pine needles to lay over this, he dragged it over to where Ulfred lay.

"Ok bro, let's get you onto it. We need to make as much speed as we can, the weather is getting worse," said Haaken scanning the incoming mist that promised ice-cold rain.

Both Haaken and Layla eased Ulfred onto the simple travois, tying him down to prevent him from rolling off.

"You will have to hold on as tight as you can buddy. Let's go."

Stepping in between the two extensions at the head of the travois, Haaken picked up the length of cord he had tied across them and ran it across the back of his neck and under his arms to form a harness.

Then he stood up, lifting Ulfred off the ground with the far end of the travois still resting on the ground.

Stepping forward with a deep grunt, Haaken set off in an awkward short stepped shuffle, his ribs protesting with every step he took. Layla followed, walking next to Ulfred. Rocky ranged ahead of them, his nose swinging from left to right scenting the frigid air as the mountain mist slowly closed in around them.

It was a good hour before Haaken managed to find the old timber road. Sweating profusely from hauling the travois over the rough terrain, Haaken now eased out of his homemade harness.

"We had better rest up for twenty minutes. At least the going will be a little easier now," he muttered.

Easing off his backpack and sitting down with his back against a pine tree, Haaken rummaged around in the pack for the bag of dry pemmican. He took out a handful, pulling the drawstring tight again with his teeth, and tossed it over to Layla and Ulfred.

"Eat guys, we need to keep going." he said.

Rocky lay at his feet, watching the handful of pemmican.

Playfully scratching the dog between his ears, Haaken took a mouthful and passed the rest to Rocky who wolfed it down in a second.

Layla fed some to Ulfred, who looked decidedly pale. The beads of sweat forming a steady line across his forehead were also cause for concern. Laying the back of her hand on his forehead, she frowned.

"Haaken, he is running quite a temperature."

CHAPTER THIRTY SEVEN

Escape To Goregate.

Arriving at Haaken's truck, Morana was sweating and out of breath, with her hair in total disarray. Wild-eyed she climbed aboard, started the vehicle, spun the tires, and sped off back along the track towards the main road.

Bouncing along at a dangerous speed on such a rough track, the diff locks whining in protest, she gripped the steering wheel tightly, knuckles gleaming white in the low light of the day. Her contorted face, a pale alabaster mask of hatred was still streaked with blood. Morana's wild eyes glared with manic insanity at the rough track ahead and the wild terrain around her. She sped along muttering constantly.

"Die! They must all die! I will have my gold mine! All the gold is mine! Mine alone!"

Her body and head bouncing violently, she drove along the track, twice skidding dangerously and bouncing off rocks and trees to help correct the sliding vehicle.

Morana eventually emerged onto the main road relatively unscathed. She slowed down knowing she had to disengage the four-wheel-drive system. Looking closely at the dashboard and almost hissing in frustration, her eyes rapidly scanned the dials and buttons. Not seeing any clues, she then focused on the gear levers.

"Aha!" The exclamation of triumph escaped from her mouth as she disengaged the four-wheel drive and sped off along the highway towards her cabin and warehouse sanctuary in Goregate.

Banging the steering wheel with a clenched fist, Morana vented her frustration with another insanely loud scream.

"Hurry, must hurry, must plan! Stupid, useless Ozil is dead! I can't trust anyone!"

Then it came to her, flitting into her mind from nowhere,

Yes! Henry you miserly old bastard! It's your fault this has gone wrong! We must chat soon! Suddenly she smiled, a gruesome visage of a pale blood-stained face staring insanely ahead as her mind now focused fully on old Henry.

The wheels of Haaken's stolen truck hummed along the highway, its powerful engine eating up the miles.

CHAPTER THIRTY EIGHT

Bear Necessities.

Haaken rose swiftly to his feet while trying to ignore the pain from his ribs and strode quickly to Ulfred's side. He was not looking well, very pale, his breathing shallow and a sheen of sweat glistening on his face.

"Okay! Let's push on before we have to stop for the night. At this slow pace we won't make it to the cabin before dark."

Stepping into his harness and lifting Ulfred, Haaken set off with grim determination to get his brother to safety. Just short of an hour later, they arrived at the smashed SUV.

Haaken stopped and eased the harness from his aching shoulders. Looking back at Layla, he spoke.

"How is he?"

"He's still with us, but struggling with a fever," replied Layla, her voice filled with worry.

Walking over to inspect the vehicle, he recoiled with shock at the horrific sight of Ozil impaled through the throat to the headrest.

"What is it?" asked Layla, noticing the backward jerk of his head as he peered into the SUV.

"It's Ozil, he's dead!" replied Haaken.

"Did she finally kill him too?" asked Layla with a weary tone, too tired to react to the news.

"No, looks like he lost control of the vehicle then rammed this tree and got impaled with a branch."

"What a terrible way to go, even if he was a slimy good for nothing," replied Layla.

Haaken called back to her,

"I must get him out. We will be warmer inside the vehicle for the night."

Wrenching open the driver's door, he calmly surveyed the bloody mess of Ozil's final demise. Moving around to the front of the vehicle, he hacked the javelin like branch pinning Ozil to the headrest off the tree with his tomahawk. It dropped loose from the tree trunk, now only supported by Ozil's throat and the seat headrest. Ozil's head appeared to nod slightly at Haaken as if in gratitude.

Haaken then took a firm grip on the branch with both hands and pulled to tear it free from Ozil and the headrest. With a gross sucking sound, the branch pulled free of the terrible wound with some of Ozil's flesh still clinging to it. Haaken tossed it aside. Returning to the open door, he wrestled Ozil's stiff body from the seat and dragged it off the timber track.

Quietly gagging and retching up bile, Layla had gone very pale as she watched Haaken tear the javelin like branch from Ozil's throat and wrestle his corpse from the SUV. Returning to her side, he laid a grubby hand on her head,

"Sorry, had to be done." he said.

She nodded her head and scrambled to her feet with a helping hand from Haaken.

"Okay, let's get Ulfred onto the back seat,"

Getting Ulfred off the travois was easier than they anticipated. He managed to stand on very weak legs and with their help, stagger across to the vehicle, ease into it, and lie down on the soft seat.

He let out a quiet sigh, feeling much warmer now out of the cold wind and misty rain. The seat was a whole lot more comfortable than Haaken's uncomfortable travois.

After clearing away the remnants of the burst airbags and getting Rocky into the rear of the vehicle, Haaken helped Layla into the passenger seat and looked into her eyes.

"We will make it. We have to. I need to get after Morana." he said.

Layla smiled at Haaken through tired eyes, her dishevelled hair framing her now much cleaner appearance. She had used a little water to clear her nose and wash herself down. Haaken looked with serious concern at her broken nose which was now twisted over to one side,

"We also have to fix your nose."

Shaking her head, Layla replied,

"No thanks, it can wait."

Haaken closed her door to keep the cold and rain out.

Turning to walk around to the driver's side door, he paused to stare at the engine. Standing there thoroughly soaked, filthy and dog tired, Haaken changed his mind and began to examine where the SUV had hit the tree.

Managing to lever the hood up with the broken limb he had earlier removed from Ozil's throat, Haaken saw that the battery was still securely in place and connected with nothing torn loose. All the cables looked fine. He leaned over to tug them gently. *Yup, still secure. Hmm. I wonder? This might just work if we can get the vehicle away from the tree first. Yes! It might just work!*

Haaken walked around to the driver's door and leaned inside to turn the ignition key. The ignition lights came on immediately. Flicking the key to the off position, he reached over and put the gear lever into neutral. The vehicle rocked back slightly as he looked up with a triumphant smile and noticed Layla watching him intently.

"You know, we might just get out of here." he said.

"What do mean?"

"Please, help me try and push the vehicle away from this tree."

Now understanding what he was up to, Layla got out and mirrored what Haaken was doing on his side. With the doors open, they both pushed hard against the door pillars to get the vehicle to move backward.

At first it wouldn't budge but then there was a small movement followed by sudden lurch. Success. They had managed to push it back a short distance away from the tree.

They looked at each other across the front seats. Haaken was smiling and he saw Layla grinning like a kid who had just found the ice cream.

"I just have to clear some of the damage from the front end before I can try to start this thing." he said.

"God, I hope it starts, Haaken", she replied.

She clambered back in and shut the door behind her, hugging her arms to herself in an effort to warm her frozen body. She was beginning to feel the effects of prolonged exposure to the bitter chill outside.

Layla watched, as Haaken eased himself around to the front end of the vehicle. *He's handling the cold better than Ulfred and I am. I'm not sure where he's getting his energy. I just feel so tired.* Watching him inspect the dented front of the SUV, she noticed him nod his head. Then he purposefully began to lever some of the bent metal outwards to free up the front of the engine. With a little more effort he cleared the dented wheel arch away from the right front wheel.

Rocky, sitting close by, watched his every move and seemed to be surveying the damage too. Haaken glanced at the dog,

"Surely this can work! Let's give it a go."

Rocky wagged his stumpy tail as if in total agreement. He followed Haaken around to the back of the vehicle and jumped inside. Haaken climbed in and turned the key. Amazingly the engine cranked over, once, twice...

"Come on, come on, please start!" he growled.

Then, amazingly, the engine started, albeit running somewhat roughly.

Quickly backing the vehicle around to face the way it had come, Haaken slowly eased off down the timber track.

Strange squeaks and knocks came from the battered front end, coupled with an uncomfortable up and down wiggle as they progressed along the track.

"Feels like something is bent on the front suspension" he said glancing at Layla "It keeps pulling to one side. Hope it gets us home,"

Layla gave him a small smile as she bounced around on her seat from the weird oscillating movement of the bent suspension. She wondered if she was going to get car sick from the constant undulating motion.

"How's Ulfred doing?" asked Haaken quietly.

"He passed out again..."

"Hang in there, bro," Haaken called back to his brother.

They wobbled slowly downwards along the wet, muddy track in the fading light. The low mist making extremely difficult to see more than a short distance in front. Twenty minutes into the journey, the broken radiator began to puff out great clouds of steam making it almost impossible to see.

"Come on, Come on! Keep going," muttered Haaken as he pictured Morana getting further and further away.

The SUV obliged valiantly and gave them another twenty minutes of tortured noise and belching steam with the stench of hot oil permeating the air. Then, suddenly, it jerked to a halt, coughed out a few clunking noises before dying with a loose rattle.

Haaken sat in silence staring straight ahead into the blanket of mist with a look of pure frustration, his jaw grinding his teeth loudly. Slowly he lifted a shaking white-knuckled fist and punched the dashboard repeatedly, venting his pent-up rage on it and roaring incoherently.

Layla jerked upright in fright at the sudden cacophony of splintering dashboard and Haaken's shouting. She was torn awake from the light sleep she had drifted into despite the bouncing of the vehicle. Laya shrank sideways against her door, fearful of getting struck by Haaken's massive fist as it pounded the dashboard.

Ulfred, semi-conscious on the back seat whimpered weakly in fear at the terrible noise coming from the front.

As suddenly as his violent wrath had exploded, it stopped, and Haaken quietly got out of the offending vehicle. Layla stared at him with wide eyes. Noticing her fearful look, Haaken spoke,

"Sorry Layla, I lost it for a moment. That bitch is getting away. Ulfred looks really bad and our best chance of making time just died."

Angrily regretting leaving his homemade travois behind, Haaken retrieved his tomahawk from the back of the vehicle. He set to work constructing another one to carry Ulfred on the final difficult haul down to the homestead.

Once again, with Ulfred secured to the travois, Haaken pulled steadily away down the wet muddy track surrounded by mist and hemmed in by pine trees. Layla followed with the rifle in one hand, battered torch in the other, trying to cast some light ahead for Haaken to navigate. Every few seconds the beam flickered badly having been damaged in the rockfall back at the mine.

The flickering torch beam cast surreal spooky shadows that seemed to dance and reach out dark twisted fingers from the trees before vanishing into the misty darkness once again. Layla shivered nervously as they played with her mind,

"Not sure how long this damned torch will hold out Haaken." she said.

"Not much we can do if it fails, Layla, but keep going. Thankfully I do know the trails and tracks around here pretty well, even in the dark."

With the dog ranging out ahead of them, Haaken and Layla trudged on through the wet misty night. Ulfred was very quiet. The only other sound above the light rain was the scraping of the travois legs carving twin grooves into the muddy timber track.

After what seemed an eternity, the log cabin appeared through the gloom, a darker shadow against the wet night. The almost flat torch batteries cast a pale weak glow on the porch railing.

Raindrops dripping from his head, Haaken halted near the porch steps, exhausted from dragging Ulfred. Breathing deeply to get more oxygen into his lungs and bone-weary body, he leaned forward to place both hands on his knees in an effort to relieve his aching shoulders. The strain of the harness pulling on them, along with the constant nagging pain from his broken made him feel like he had been dragging Ulfred along for days.

Layla stepped forward, casting the feeble torch beam onto the front door, then stopped.

Rocky started to growl, this time a very different growl, a deep threatening rumble from his barrel chest. Haaken slowly raised his weary head.

"Haaken, the front door is open!" Layla cried out in alarm.

Just then, an incredibly large brown form burst from the open door of the cabin with a roar that seemed to reverberate through the trees. A blast of hot, fetid air washed over them as the terrible sound of rage announced the promise of a swift death. The creature bounded off the porch and struck Haaken who was struggling to get out of the travois harness. It then turned swiftly and knocked Rocky flying with a potent swipe of its massive clawed paw.

The Grizzly Bear roared again, its massive lips shaking with the volume of air rushing out of its large wide-open mouth, exposing huge canines as it spun back to the travois scenting the semi-conscious and blood-covered Ulfred.

Now wide awake and still tied to the travois, Ulfred stared up in absolute horror and disbelief while a terrible mewling sound escaped his lips. At that precise moment, the Grizzly, with one mind-blowingly powerful swipe of its dinner-plate-sized paw and long claws, hooked Ulfred by the head and ripped him from the travois. It flicked him over onto his face in the mud like a rag doll with half his scalp torn off, exposing the white bone of his skull. The monster of a bear stepped over the travois to bounce heavily with both front paws on Ulfred's back. The irate bear tore into the flesh of Ulfred's back with its long sharp claws, savagely biting deeply into his back and shoulders before spinning about and quickly disappearing into the forest.

Time seemed to stand still. Each second felt like an eternity for Haaken who was lying flat on his back, and for Layla, who had dropped both the torch and the rifle when the bear had burst from the cabin.

Just as suddenly, time returned to normal, as Haaken scrambled to his feet. Layla picked up the rifle and fired two rounds towards the forest in the direction the grizzly had sped off.

Haaken leapt towards Ulfred, shouting out to him with pure desperation in his eyes. He feared his brother was done for.

"Ulfred, Ulfred!" he cried.

Dropping to his knees with a look of pure horror on his face, he stared at Ulfred's blood-soaked shoulders, torn scalp, and savaged back. *Oh God, please be alive. Gently,* he turned his brother over.

Ulfred gasped for air, his whole body shaking violently, eyes wide open in a wild blank stare. A terrible, soul destroying sound of pure terror broke forth from his bleeding lips.

Haaken turned to look at Layla who was staring into the forest with the rifle still at her shoulder, steadily aiming at where the wild beast had vanished.

"Are you okay, Layla?" he said.

She didn't move, and appeared frozen in place. Haaken called again, this time louder, in a commanding voice,

"Layla!" still she did not move "The bear has gone!"

Layla jerked back to reality, turning to stare at Haaken, her face ashen, her mouth trembling, as she tried to speak. The terrible shock of the speed at which the bear had attacked still registered in her eyes.

In a calm measured tone, Haaken spoke slowly and clearly to her,

"Layla, please help me get Ulfred inside now."

She quietly walked over to the porch to place the rifle against the railing and then turned to squat down by Ulfred's side to gently lift him up. Once they managed to get him upright, Haaken bent to pick his brother up and carry him across his shoulders in a fireman's lift.

Wearily Haaken mounted the steps, with Layla leading the way into the main room of the cabin. Rocky followed closely on Haaken's heels, still growling deeply. The place was in a complete shambles with household items scattered and furniture overturned and ripped apart. Fortunately, the large dining table was still standing. Layla quickly cleared it, to let Haaken lay his critically traumatised brother on it.

Taking Haaken by his arm in the direction of the large fireplace, Layla looked up at him with tears in her eyes.

"I'm so, so sorry, Haaken." she said.

"You must light the fire. We need to warm him up, as well as ourselves. The warmth will help him. I also need hot water to clean his wounds and lots of hot coffee, with heaps of sugar."

Haaken blinked his eyes to clear the fog of events looping across his mind in slow motion. Eventually they cleared and Layla came into sharp focus, looking up at him. Slowly he reached out a large muddy hand to her face and lightly ran his finger down her soft grubby cheek.

"Thank you, Layla," he said in a low gravelly voice.

His words were deep with emotion, and something much more. With a tight feeling in her chest, Layla instinctively knew.

Haaken turned on his heels to go and secure the front door. Then he went quietly over to squat before the fireplace to place kindling and logs in it. Within a few minutes the fire was roaring, throwing out much-needed heat across the cold room. Rocky had stretched out in front of the flames, soaking up the heat with his eyes closed. Soon Haaken had lit several hurricane lamps, spreading light to every corner of the room.

Layla had dug up a large metal bowl, filled it with fresh water, and placed it on the old wood stove to heat up. A pot of coffee was beginning to steam up alongside it. Casting her eyes about the room with a questioning look on her face, she said,

"Have you got anything to clean him up with? And bandages"

Now focused again, Haaken quickly retrieved his emergency medical box and placed it on the table next to Ulfred. He brought the large bowl of hot water to the table, leaving another on the stove to heat up.

They both set to the grim task of stripping Ulfred and cleaning his wounds. Ulfred lay still, like a cold, pale corpse on the table. Several times they checked his feeble pulse. It was still there, only just, but there.

Working in silence, they cleaned the wounds as best they could. Both were deeply shocked at the severity of Morana's sadistic torture on his bruised, battered and mutilated body.

The bear had also inflicted terrible wounds, deep penetrating holes from its teeth and horrible deep slash wounds from its long claws exposing the ribs along Ulfred's back. It had also torn and ripped his scalp. His entire body was mutilated.

Having used up all the antiseptic in the medical kit, Haaken now focused on his brother's head. Ulfred's terrible head wound proved the most difficult to deal with. The bear's massive claws had ripped three deep grooves across the top of Ulfred's skull, lifting the scalp totally off his head leaving three large loose flaps of skin and hair hanging loosely off his head.

Haaken knew he must first sew the skin together where he could. He would then have to sew it back to the flesh on the sides of his brother's head, to at least partially cover the raw scalp. Frowning with concentration, he set to work, using a simple blanket stitch to bring the edges of the skin together.

Watching in morbid fascination, Layla stood rooted to the spot, the odd heave threatening to make her vomit into the bloody water in the steel bowl next to her.

Finally, they had done as much as they could for Ulfred. After wrapping him in warm blankets, Haaken stood very still, the tears in his fierce hazel eyes reflecting the deep emotional pain in his heart for what his brother had endured.

Now driven to the very edge of his own sanity, Haaken looked down at his comatose brother, his mind's eye vividly replaying the terrible, visible trauma carried out on his brother's pale body.

With arms shaking, he gripped the table tightly, and in a low menacing voice, tight with incredible anger, he spoke.

"May the hounds of hell, baying for blood, give me the strength to find the bitch and rip her disgusting, poisonous soul from her body.

God have mercy on her soul, for I will never forgive her or anyone else on this planet for such vile evilness."

Layla looked up, shocked, but truly understanding Haaken's deep emotional outburst.

CHAPTER THIRTY NINE

Morana's Cabin.

Arriving at last in Goregate, her eyes still intense with manic hatred, Morana Renwick drove through the town on her way up the mountain road to her cabin.

Sitting at his table in the dining room of the Hotel Hope, old Henry observed Haaken's Ford Bronco pass by at speed, with only one occupant. With a puzzled look on his face, Henry thought. *That's very strange, why would he be heading out to the old mine and Morana's cabin?*

Halfway through town, Morana decided to stop at the warehouse, her vile mind swirling with an intensity of terrible plans and her immediate needs. *Must get my money and jewellery. It's mine, all mine! Must put it in a safer place! Then plan their demise. Oh Yes! Such a pleasure it will be!*

Skidding to a stop outside the door to the warehouse, Morana quickly entered and proceeded upstairs to the office.

With frantic, wildly animated movements, she set about clearing out her ill-gotten gains starting with the huge pile of cash neatly stacked in the large safe. She then proceeded to haul out the many other valuable items from the safe - gifts from cleverly blackmailed clients. There were piles of gold rings, diamond bracelets and beautiful necklaces studded with fabulous diamonds and other expensive stones, along with many other smaller items of costume jewellery.

Now and then a shrill, deranged cackle burst forth from her lips as she hastily stuffed it all into two large leather bags with heavy-duty zips. In her haste she dropped several thousand dollars and some loose jewellery on the floor before zipping up the bags and staggering back to Haaken's Bronco, grunting under the weight.

Tossing the heavy bags onto the back seat, her bloodshot eyes still staring wildly out of her face, Morana's wildly fluctuating mind suddenly turned to Henry. *Yes! Henry will come with me. It's his idea. It's his damn fault this has gone wrong!* With an twisted smile of ugly malice, she spun the steering wheel and sped off back to the Hotel Hope.

The rapid spinning of the old rotating door seemed to spit her out into the foyer in front of old Henry who was slowly sweeping the floor with an ancient broom. The mangy black cat rose vertically off the wooden bench, hissing wildly with legs extended stiffly. Its claws were fully extended and its hair stood out like porcupine quills before it fled with a fearful screech.

Shocked at seeing her appear in front of him, her auburn hair in wild disarray around a pale white blood-stained face with manic looking eyes, Henry staggered back a few paces, fearful for his life.

Reaching out a strong arm, Morana locked her hand into his shirt front and jerked him towards her. Angrily spraying spittle into his face, she shouted loudly,

"You useless old man, Haaken Hunter has ruined everything and he is coming after me. You are going to help me stop him when he gets here!"

His eyes wide with shock at her violent outburst, Henry struggled to breathe with her choking hand twisted into his shirt front. He gasped hoarsely,

"Wha... Wha... What are you talking about, Morana?"

Dragging him by the shirt out to the Bronco, she shoved him into the front passenger seat and slammed the door. Morana ran around to the other side of the vehicle and jumped into the driver's seat. They sped off towards her cabin up at the old gold mine. A terrible silence, pregnant with tension, filled the cab.

Henry's watery old eyes glanced nervously at Morana as she drove at break neck speed up the road. *Lord help me, I think she's finally gone completely round the bend, and why is she driving Haaken's truck?* Slowly, a cunning thought crept into his mind. *Maybe I took too much for granted when I believed she could pull this off and get us the gold. I think I will have to stop her before she does something to me!* He turned his head to stare out at the road ahead.

Sliding the truck to a stop outside her cabin, Morana leapt out and pulled Henry violently from the vehicle then marched him inside and sat him down at the kitchen table. As she paced up and down in front of him, her wicked mind was already sewing together a devious plan to trap Haaken Hunter and kill him.

Smiling sweetly at old Henry, and now holding his hand, she spoke in dulcet tones,

"Listen, uncle Henry. I'm really sorry I just shouted at you and treated you so roughly. But I'm at the end of my tether. It all went so horribly wrong up there at the Hunter homestead and the Double H mine. You know I trust you completely, you have always been there for me."

Morana gently squeezed his hand, looking deeply into his eyes with a sweet, innocent look on her pale blood-stained face.

Looking up at her with a puzzled look on his face, he realized then how dangerous she could be. Henry simply nodded his head slowly in quiet agreement.

"Henry..." she said "You know these old mine workings better than anyone else. You must help me get prepared. You need to guide me underground into the old mine. We need to hide out there for a day or two. Firstly we will hide his truck, and then we will go into the mine. Surely you must remember a few places we can safely hide out at. Deep enough into the mine, where nobody will find us."

Henry stared at her in horror. He hated the place. She continued excitedly, now caught up in her plan, her arms gesticulating wildly,

"Haaken will come. He will check the hotel and warehouse before he gets up here to the cabin. It won't take him long to figure out we have left. Yes! I have some maps over by the bureau. I'll leave one of them open with some nearby towns marked on it and he will figure that's where we are going. After a day or two, we can come out. While we are hiding, we will figure out a way to lay a trap for him. We must kill him and then the Double H will be ours."

Smiling at her own plan, Morana thumped the kitchen table with excitement and a manic look in her eyes.

Henry's hands had begun to shake more than usual,

"But Morana, it's not safe down there. They condemned the place years ago. Rockfalls happen all the time there!"

Taking Henry by both his hands, Morana looked deep into his eyes with a radiant smile on her dirty face, still stained with dried blood. She purred quietly in a soothing voice,

"My dear Uncle Henry, you know I love you, we can do this together, I will keep you safe, don't worry."

Despite his misgivings, Henry could not help but feel warmed by her apparent feelings for him. No one had uttered such words of endearment to him for years. He had almost forgotten what they sounded like. Smiling weakly into her eyes, he found himself happily nodding his head in total agreement with her.

Morana gently squeezed his hands and then hugged Henry while she stared over his shoulder at the kitchen door.

You stupid old imbecile. Once this is over, you are going to pay dearly.

CHAPTER FORTY

A Time To Die

Haaken and Layla both collapsed, completely exhausted, onto the large old leather sofa.

"We need to keep checking on Ulfred. I'll take the first shift. You try and get some sleep" he said.

Too tired to argue, Layla nestled her head on his shoulder and fell into a deep, dreamless sleep.

Haaken stared into the flames of the fire, watching the wild, surreal shapes of the flames as they danced for a moment then disappeared to be instantly replaced by more. To his weary eyes and exhausted mind, some of them appeared to reach out with demonic, grotesque faces to mock him. His mind wrestled with not being able to stop Morana before she escaped from his father's mine. His eyes drooped lower and his chin slowly sank onto his chest. Jerking his head up suddenly, he forced himself to focus on the flames, but his chin dropped again to his chest. Haaken slept.

Abruptly Haaken opened his eyes. The fire had died down to hot glowing embers. *Shit! I fell asleep!* He looked down to where Layla had been lying but she was not there. Alarmed, he struggled to his feet, stretched his arms while calling out quietly,

"Layla?"

"I'm here, Haaken, by Ulfred," she replied, sipping from a hot cup of coffee.

"How is he?" Haaken asked with concern as he walked over to the stove to pour himself a cup of coffee.

"Not good, Haaken," replied, Layla quietly.

Haaken quickly walked over to where she stood by Ulfred's side. Looking down at him, he thought grimly, *My God, he is so pale*. Reaching out a hand, he laid it against Ulfred's sweat covered brow.

"He feels so cold and clammy."

Ulfred Hunter was gravely ill. His chest barely moved as his weak, ragged breathing struggled to keep him going.

Layla looked at Haaken with tears in her eyes.

"I don't know if he will make it to the morning!" she whispered.

Closing his eyes, Haaken growled,

"He has to. We have much to talk about."

He swallowed his hot coffee and walked back to the fireplace to put some more logs on the embers. Haaken stared out of the window as the darkness outside began to give way to a new day. The rays of the sun reaching out to banish the night with the pale pink light of dawn.

Suddenly, Ulfred called out, in a strong clear voice,

"Haaken, Where are you Haaken!?"

Leaping over a chair lying on its side, Haaken called out,

"I'm here, brother."

With a weak smile, Ulfred looked up at Haaken,

"I'm sorry, Haaken."

Beginning to shake his head, Haaken opened his mouth to talk. Ulfred feebly fluttered a hand,

"Please let me finish..." he said "It's important. I know I was wrong to leave the way I did. It was stupid, impetuous arrogance. I hope you can forgive me, my brother, for bringing all this trouble home. I know what our father did was wrong. He should have told us we had different mothers."

His mind wandered briefly before he carried on speaking,

"How can, someone so evil, be my sister. Be careful of her, Haaken. She is insane. I thought I loved her. No, that's wrong, I do love her - how weird is that? But how can that be possible."

"It's okay, Ulfred. You did what you thought was right for you. There is no need to forgive you for anything you have done. I do understand why you left. Now, let's get you better so we can work together from there."

Ulfred smiled weakly at his brother's concern,

"I'm scared, Haaken. I don't want to die now."

"You are not going to die!" said Haaken "I love you, Ulfred. You fight this, do you hear me!"

Ulfred lifted his mutilated hand weakly to lightly grip Haaken's wrist and smiled up at him in understanding,

"I'm so sorry my brother."

Ulfred let go of his last breath. His hand fell from Haaken's wrist onto the table and his head rolled gently to the side.

Haaken could not see through the flood of tears that threatened to consume him. An overwhelming tide of emotion seemed to choke his very desire to breathe.

Haaken Hunter roared at the world with a bellow so loud the roof timbers rattled. His grief was mind-numbing in its intensity.

Layla's cup of coffee crashed to the floor, smashing into hundreds of pieces, like the scattered remnants of Haakens feelings.

Struggling to breathe, his two broken ribs reminding him of so much pain and ugliness, Haaken looked silently at his brother's battered face, now so serene and peaceful.

You will burn, bitch! His thought screamed across the empty space of time, reaching out to Morana. He turned to Layla, an ice-cold look of grim determination on his face.

"We must prepare a place next to our mother for him."

He bent down to place a kiss on Ulfred's forehead, before calmly closing his lifeless eyes.

Then, just as calmly, he walked outside to find a spade to prepare Ulfred's grave, closely followed by Rocky who shadowed his every move.

With tears running down her face, Layla wrapped Ulfred's body up as best she could with the blanket. Her mind was numb from the recent chaotic and tragic events. Time stood still again for Layla. It seemed that Haaken had no sooner left with the spade when he reappeared at the door.

Still silent and pale, his face was set like stone. Quietly he went to Ulfred and lifted his brother onto his shoulders.

Layla followed him outside and up the slope to the family burial plot behind the cabin.

The smell of the freshly turned earth, mixed with the pure scent of pine needles permeated the early morning air. Silent tendrils of mist floated across the open space like soft gentle hands welcoming Ulfred to his final resting place.

CHAPTER FORTY ONE

Morana And Henry

Her madness knew no bounds. Morana hid the Bronco a short distance into the forest, not far from the cabin along the loop road. She stashed her ill-gotten wealth in the leather bags behind the front seat. She cleverly covered the truck with piles of leafy branches to conceal it before returning for Henry.

Morana pushed Henry ahead of her as they entered the old mine. He staggered a little, feeling weak from lack of sleep. She had kept him up all night. With the light from her torch shining the way ahead, they disappeared into the bowels of the earth. Henry was sweating nervously as they proceeded into the dark, damp tunnels. He truly hated the place. It brought back so many old and terrible memories.

After a good twenty minutes of stumbling along the rotting rail line and carefully avoiding the rockfalls, Henry guided them into a shallow cut out area in the sidewall of the tunnel. Morana viewed the remnants of the small electrical workshop with disdain. Lying scattered about were parts of machinery, some lying in small pools of water, others rusting away in the damp atmosphere. This was all that what was left of a once clean and efficient electrical workshop for the mine electricians.

Henry wearily sank down, to sit on a rusting toolbox with his chest making an eerie, wheezing sound every time he drew a deep breath.

"I must rest, Morana!"

Eyeing him with an angry frown creasing her forehead, Morana reluctantly agreed.

"Only for a short while, Henry."

Despite the cold dampness of the place, Henry dozed off, exhausted from his forced march into the mine. Morana paced up and down for a while before settling herself on a bent, four-legged stool.

CHAPTER FORTY TWO

Farewell.

Standing silently at Ulfred's graveside, now neatly filled in beside their mother's grave, Haaken felt numb. Arms hanging straight down by his sides, fists clenching and unclenching, he had no words to express himself.

Sensing he was struggling to find something to say, Layla took hold of his hand and held it with both of hers. Rocky, who was sitting patiently nearby, got up to stand at Haaken's side. Haaken opened his clenched fist and gently rested it on top of Rocky's large broad head.

Clearing his throat several times, Haaken spoke quietly,

"It's time…"

They left the small family graveside and quietly returned to the cabin. Once there, Haaken paused on the porch steps to light his first Cohiba of the day. He turned his head to look down the track leading to the valley below, tendrils of fragrant smoke drifting from his nostrils. The fresh woody scent of pine bark filled the air, accompanied by the peaceful sound of the mountain stream nearby as it bubbled and gurgled along on its journey down to the valley.

Haaken frowned as the sound of a vehicle slowly making its way up the rough track to the cabin drifted up on the clear mountain air. The dog growled quietly, and the hair on the back of his neck rose.

Déjà Vu Haaken! His restless mind rolled out the words like a ticker-tape sign as a loud backfire from the struggling vehicle rent the air. The chickens cackled in alarm as they wandered freely about having escaped the clutches of the bear which had destroyed their pen.

The tension left his shoulders, as he recognised the sound of Georgio's truck. Haaken called out to Layla who was trying to clean up some of the mess inside.

"Layla.." he said "Georgio is on his way up in his old rattletrap of a truck. We can get a ride back down to the store with him."

Layla came to the door just as Georgio pulled up with another backfire belching out a cloud of black exhaust fumes as he turned off the ignition.

Almost rolling his large rotund frame from the vehicle, Georgio waddled up to the porch on his bandy legs, a big smile lighting up his face. His words tumbled out in between wheezy deep breaths and he spoke in a relieved tone,

"Haaken, my friend, how are you? I have been so worried. No sign or message from you. Are you okay?"

Spotting Layla at the door, he cheerfully waved a pudgy hand,

"Hello, Ma'am."

Clumping up the porch steps, Georgio plonked his large body down on the wooden bench near the front door which creaked loudly in protest. Layla reappeared with two mugs of hot coffee for them. Georgio was no fool, despite his bluff manner.

"What's going on my friend?" he asked "I saw your Bronco flying past my store and it was definitely not you driving. So I'm thinking to myself, Georgio, you better get yourself up to Haaken's cabin, something is wrong."

Easing his weary body carefully down onto the bench next to Georgio, Haaken told him the whole story right up to the present moment. Shocked into absolute silence, Georgio grabbed his St. Christopher and kissed it several times, shaking his head in disbelief.

"Haaken, my friend. My heart hurts for you, Ulfred, and your father. I am truly sorry to hear this terrible news."

He paused for breath

"Anything, I mean anything you want, it is yours. I can help."

"Thank you, Georgio" said Haaken "You are a good friend. We do need help to get to Goregate as quickly as possible. I have to stop this woman."

"Consider it done..." came the reply "I have a vehicle parked at the back of my store. You can borrow it for as long as you need it and take anything you need from my store to hunt down this devil of a woman!"

Georgio superstitiously spat on the porch floor and kissed his St Christopher once again.

Haaken jumped to his feet,

"We will be ready to go in a few minutes."

Georgio simply nodded his head, heaved his large bulk up from the bench, and headed back to his truck to wait.

Haaken and Layla grabbed their packs and secured the cabin properly. Taking Layla's pack from her, Haaken hopped into the back of the truck with Rocky while Layla sat upfront with Georgio. With another loud backfire, the truck started and they bounced and rattled off along the track down the mountain to Solitude and Georgio's store. With one large hand resting on Rocky sitting next to him, Haaken stared at the passing forest and the mountains as they descended to the valley below.

Once again life's events had somehow found a way to destroy the peaceful sanctity of his homestead and quiet tranquil life.

CHAPTER FORTY THREE

The Hunt Begins.

After stocking up on a few essential items, Haaken, Layla, and Rocky set off for Goregate in Georgio's pride and joy. A fully restored 1952 Chevy 3100 truck. Many hours later they pulled up outside The Slaughtered Lamb. Layla let them into the kitchen where Haaken immediately sat down at the long wooden kitchen table to check over the contents of his backpack. *Torch, nylon cord, nylon rope, water, tomahawk, broken bowie knife, boot knife, a bag of pemmican, spare batteries.* Layla sat quietly with a look of concern on her face as she watched him prepare. With a satisfied grunt, Haaken stood up and shouldeed his pack before looking across at Layla and speaking in his gravelly voice,

"I have to finish this on my own...."

"I know you do, Haaken, but please be careful. She is so dangerous."

"I know she is..." he replied with a tight smile.

Turning on his heels, Haaken left with Rocky following close by. The dog bounded into the cab of the Chevy to sit next to him as Haaken started the engine and drove the short distance to The Hotel Hope. *I need to collect old Henry first.*

Pulling up outside, he left Rocky in the vehicle and pushed through the worn revolving door into the foyer. Stopping just inside, he carefully surveyed the entire room. The mangy-looking black cat lay on the old wooden bench glaring through green eyes at him. Henry's broom lay on the floor where it had fallen from his hands when Morana had arrived to snatch him away.

Only silence greeted Haaken. *Looks like she took the old man with her.* He quickly left the hotel and proceeded with haste to the warehouse, safely parking some distance away.

Haaken and Rocky carefully entered the open doorway into the darkened warehouse. Watching the dog, Haaken could see no reaction from him. *I don't think anyone is here, but I'd better check the office upstairs.* He moved quickly and quietly across the vast floor area of the warehouse and up the stairs to the mezzanine floor. Entering the office he found the few scattered bank notes and items of loose jewellery that Morana had dropped on the floor in her haste. The safe door was wide open.

"Already made off with her stolen wealth, buddy," Haaken muttered aloud to Rocky who was sniffing about with his hackles up.

A low growling rumble vibrated from his chest at the scent of Morana in the room.

"Come on, Rocky, we'd better get up to her cabin!" he called as he bounded down the metal stairs and out to the parked truck.

The dog trailed happily after him.

CHAPTER FORTY FOUR

Lost.

Morana's head snapped up as her tired eyes focused in the dim darkness around her. Henry's sleeping face was eerily lit up by the torch next to him, now only lit by a dim glow. He had obviously left it on.

Jumping up with her nerves on edge, she walked over to Henry and kicked his feet, shouting,

"Henry! We need to go deeper!"

Jerking awake, Henry was blinded by her bright torchlight shining into his face.

"No, Morana, this is far enough...The place could come down on our heads at any time." he protested in a squeaky voice, looking about nervously.

Morana cuffed him across the back of his head,

"Grow some balls you weak old fool. We go on!"

Forcing him onwards, they came to a three-way branch in the main tunnel.

"Which way do we go, Henry?"

Henry dithered about, scratching his head and whining loudly,

"It's been such a long time since I've been down here, I'm not sure."

Morana pushed roughly him towards the smaller tunnel bearing off to the right. It was at that moment that the old man realized. *She isn't, calling me Uncle anymore.*

They both stumbled off into the darkness with their torch beams - one weak, one strong, wavering about erratically as they slowly made their way ever deeper into the rotting mine.

CHAPTER FORTY FIVE

Cabin In The Woods.

Haaken skidded Georgio's pristine Chevy truck to a halt outside Morana's Cabin, flung open the door, and jumped from the cab. Sensing Haaken's rising tension and urgency, Rocky pushed around him and ran into the cabin through the open kitchen door.

"Shit! Rocky, wait!" Haaken called out, as he ran after the dog into the kitchen half expecting to find the bitch waiting for him.

Nobody was there. Only silence greeted him with the scent of stale smoke from the dead log fire tainted with a hint of Chanel no 5. Casting about for any clues, Haaken began rummaging about the room until he saw the maps open on the old writing bureau. He noticed the scribbled markings on the maps around a few nearby towns and cities. *Fucking Hell! Don't tell me they have left for one of these places.*

Angrily Haaken swept the maps to the floor then realised that Rocky had left the cabin.

"Rocky? Where the hell have you gone?" Haaken called out irritably.

Calm down man, think! Quietly Haaken moved from the cabin and stood outside the kitchen next to the tool shed. He spotted Rocky walking slowly along the loop road with his nose to the ground. Moving silently along the road, Haaken caught up with the dog as he trotted off the road and carried on into the tree line.

Looking down at the ground, Haaken could see the recent tracks of the vehicle heading off the road. Now, more than intrigued, he followed them to find Rocky sitting next to his Bronco, which had been carefully camouflaged with piles of branches. Ruffling the big dog's head, Haaken said quietly,

"She is devious, Rocky. Trying to fool us into thinking they have got away by hiding the truck."

Squatting down with his arm around the big dog's neck, he spoke again,

"I'll bet they're hiding in the mine. What do you think?"

Rocky licked his hand, then stood up, sniffing the air as he stepped forward.

"We had better get my pack and find out..." Haaken said they both trotted back to the Chevy.

Haaken went back quickly to collect his backpack as Rocky kept moving towards the old mine, stopping short of the entrance and growling with his hackles up.

Haaken quickly shouldered his pack and followed, gently patting the dog while talking quietly in his gravelly voice,

"Yup, they're in there. Probably set a trap for us too!"

CHAPTER FORTY SIX

What Goes Around.

Morana and old Henry had not progressed very far into the smaller side tunnel when Henry stumbled on some loose rocks and fell headlong into some rotten timber supports, upsetting a couple of them.

An ominous crack sounded, closely followed by a loud drawn-out creak. Suddenly the rotten timber support snapped with a loud report similar to a pistol going off. The badly fractured tunnel roof suddenly caved in. Several large slabs of rock fell from the tunnel roof, cruelly trapping Henry's lower body beneath an enormous pile of broken rock. Henry's high pitched scream echoed wildly off the rock walls as his hands frantically beat and pushed against the weight bearing down on him. His crushed pelvis drove hot rods of intense pain through his body and into his tortured mind.

Morana shrieked in terror as heavy rocks knocked her to the floor, trapping one of her arms. The pain sent her into a manic frenzy of insane anger,

"Henry! You dumb, stupid, fucking idiot! Look what you've done!" she shrieked.

Henry's torch, now crushed beneath a huge slab of rock, was no longer working. The only light in the dust-filled tunnel came from Morana's torch which had fallen near where she lay. Stretching out her free arm, she could not quite reach it. Turning back to her trapped arm, Morana went berserk, screeching and screaming as she tugged violently at her own arm. Suddenly the arm pulled loose and she fell back, striking her head hard on the unforgiving rock floor. In a daze she grabbed her torch, then she shone it on her torn arm. Another terrible scream rent the dusty air, echoing along the tunnel. The razor-sharp rock, falling like a guillotine onto her hand had been unmerciful. It had silently severed four fingers from her hand.

Henry lay on his back, twitching and moaning with a trickle of blood running from the side of his mouth. He stared up at her mutilated hand as it seemed to loom out of the darkness in the bright beam of her torch. Short jets of blood pulsed from it with every beat of her evil heart.

Placing the torch on the floor, Morana frantically tore one-handed at her expensive blouse, managing to rip a piece off. She clumsily bound her hand using both her teeth and her good hand to pull the rough bandage tight enough to slow the flow of blood.

Pale and panting from the effort, she now had a very real, new-found, and deep-seated fear of her own mutilation. Morana screamed aloud again, venting her deranged anger at the dark, dusty mine tunnel. Picking up her torch, and leaping to her feet, Morana shrieked once again. At that moment she bolted back down the tunnel, abandoning old Henry to his own fate. Her wild, cackling laughter echoed off the tunnel walls as total darkness enveloped Henry in its cold embrace.

CHAPTER FORTY SEVEN

The Reckoning – Part One

Still standing outside the old mine entrance, Rocky stepped back a little, whining quietly. Then a low growl began to rumble deep inside his chest.

The sudden rumble from the tunnel entrance and the tremors he felt through his feet announced ominously to Haaken that there had been a rockfall deep inside the mine.

Standing with Rocky at the entrance to the mine, Haaken could feel an extra bite to the chilled air blowing in ahead of the massive cold front bearing down from the North. It drove icy fingers down the back of his neck while his latent fear of enclosed, dark places popped cold sweat across his brow.

Torch in hand, Haaken set off into the mine with Rocky at his heels. Wary of an ambush or trap, they made their way with caution, deeper and deeper into the mine along the dark dank treacherous tunnel.

After a slow but cautious walk, they arrived at the three-way branch and Haaken flicked his torch from one tunnel to the other in an effort to decide which way to go. Rocky solved the problem by staring down the smaller tunnel on the right. Moving along it, Haaken carefully picked his way over the loose rock and rubble before coming to an abrupt stop when he heard the wheezing rattle of laboured breathing together with painful groaning.

Haaken inched his way forward to find, caught in the light of his torch, old Henry cruelly trapped from his waist down beneath the rockfall. His pale, blood-stained face was staring at Morana's severed fingers which lay on the tunnel floor not far from him. The harsh glare of the torch reflected off the blood-red nail polish painted on each pale alabaster-white finger.

Swinging the beam away from Henry's bloodshot, watery eyes, Haaken saw no sign of Morana. Slowly, he squatted down next to Henry's face. Henry looked up at him, a desperate look in his eyes as he gasped weakly,

"Help me, please!"

His face as cold as the stone walls surrounding them, Haaken quietly spoke,

"As ye sow, so shall ye reap, Henry!"

With a puzzled look on his face, Henry shook his head silently. Haaken spoke again, just as quietly,

"You left my father to die the same fate, Henry. Trapped and alone in his mine."

Henry gasped aloud. A little more blood trickled from the side of his mouth as the realisation dawned in his aged eyes.

"Yes Henry! I know what you did!" said Haaken coldly as he stood up.

Henry's mouth worked in silent desperation. He reached out a trembling hand to touch Haaken's boot before he managed to speak again in a weak, trembling voice,

"Please forgive me, Haaken. I was a different person back then. I was greedy, only thinking of myself and the gold. I'm different now. I know what I did was wrong…"

Haaken stood silently, staring down at the dying old man bathed in the light thrown off the tunnel walls and rockpile.

"Don't go Haaken, I'm all alone." Henry pleaded

Haaken replied, his voice as cold as ice.

"And so it should be Henry. Just you and God. Make your peace, he will judge you."

He turned and walked away to search for Morana.

Total darkness descended upon Henry as he whimpered away his last moments, totally alone.

CHAPTER FORTY EIGHT

The Reckoning – Part Two

Moving as quietly as possible, Haaken and Rocky carefully made their way back along the narrow shaft towards the main tunnel. *Where are you hiding, Morana?*

Worried that she might be making her escape, he picked up his pace casting aside the thought of her lying in wait to ambush him.

Suddenly Rocky stopped, the hackles from his neck to his short stumpy tail standing stiffly while a low growl erupted from him. Almost falling over the dog, Haaken slid to a stop. Listening intently, he turned his torch off, deliberately shutting out his fear of the smothering darkness.

Then he heard it. The sound was coming from somewhere up ahead. A scrabbling sound of something or someone trying to find purchase on a difficult surface. At the same time, a hideous, primal sound rose and fell with desperation causing the very air to quiver. Haaken's hair stood on end. Wide-eyed, he flicked on his torch but could see nothing ahead. There was only that horrible sound.

Now, creeping forward with Rocky close by his side, Haaken searched ahead of them with the bright beam of the torch. After what felt like an eternity he saw another tunnel branching away at an angle from the narrow shaft they were in. Realising how easy it would be to take the wrong route and get lost forever, Haaken was grateful to have Rocky with him.

Together they crept slowly along the new tunnel. Haaken could now quite clearly hear the strange noise coming from somewhere up ahead in the darkness beyond the beam of his torch. The sound of angry snuffling and deep throaty grunting coupled with high pitched moaning grew louder and more desperate the closer they got to it.

Taking great care as he negotiated the rockfalls, Haaken suddenly came to a stop and instantly broke out in a cold sweat at the sight in front of him. A ghostly alabaster white face with wild hate-filled eyes glared into the beam of his torch from floor level. His mind balked in horror. *What the fuck is that? Holy shit! It's Morana!* Calming down somewhat, he studied her quietly in the torchlight.

Morana had gotten lost, when in her violent blind panic to escape the mine, she had mistakenly taken the wrong tunnel and fallen into an ore dumping shaft. Fortunately for her, she had managed to grab the crumbling edge of the deep shaft to stop herself from immediately plunging to the bottom of the shaft. It was forty feet deep with the bottom of the shaft sealed off by a set of large rusted steel grizzly bars set above an old rock jaw crusher.

His face an ice-cold mask of stone, Haaken quietly spoke,

"Hello, Morana,"

Her frantic foot scrabbling against the worn vertical rock wall of the ore shaft increased. Her red lips parted in a snarl with the lipstick smeared on her teeth making her pale face look like a bizarre mask of horror rising up from the very depths of hell.

She hung from her one good hand, now a raw bleeding claw with the fingernails torn off and buried up to the knuckles in a narrow crack in the floor. Morana still managed to spit her vindicitive, malicious hatred at him.

Haaken could hear her finger joints popping from the strain of supporting her body. The only thing that prevented Morana from letting go and plunging down the shaft to an abrupt and bloody stop on the ugly rusty steel bars below was her sheer manic fury at her present predicament. She desperately clung, one-handed, while the blood-soaked, cloth bound stumped remains of her other hand flailed blindly for a handhold on the crumbling ledge of the shaft. But it was an impossible task.

Haaken slowly approached the edge of the shaft, weary of it collapsing under his extra weight. The closer he got, the more she hissed and spat her vitriolic hatred at him and his family while staring blindly into the bright torch beam.

Still frothing at the mouth she screamed,

"I hate you, Haaken Hunter. And your family. The gold and money are mine! Your father owes it all to me for his lies!"

Quietly ignoring her, Haaken sat down close to where she clung so desperately to the edge of the shaft with her one hand. He reached into his top pocket and took out an unfinished Cohiba. Still not saying a word, he lit up his cigar, took a quiet draw, then slowly expelled a cloud of sweet-smelling smoke at the far wall of the tunnel. Rocky edged a little closer, standing alert with his eyes focused on

Morana's head while a low rumble of anger vibrated in his barrel of a chest. The scent of Morana, an ugly reminder of his own painful abuse.

"Easy, Rocky," commanded Haaken.

The big dog sat down to watch. Haaken swung the bright torch beam away from her eyes. No longer blinded by the light, Morana could now see Haaken clearly. Her lips twisted upwards into a hideous semblance of a smile. Even while hanging on for dear life she still managed to inject a note of sensual lust into her voice.

"I can make your life richer, Haaken. Help me up. I can show you so many ways to wealth and pleasure. We will be good together."

"No, Morana..." he replied coldly "You are an evil, malignant tumour. A vile, cursed monster from hell. You are only capable of inflicting pain and agony before sucking the life from your victims. Your savage, insatiable lust will never be satisfied."

In an instant she spat towards him, her spittle half hanging from her twisted lips as she screamed like a deranged banshee. Haaken got to his feet to look down at this sight of such incomprehensible evil. Quietly, he spoke once again in his gravelly voice,

"Morana, I came to kill you for what you did to my brother. Ulfred loved life itself. He would never harm a soul, yet you chose to inflict such unimaginable pain and suffering on him. He is, and always will be my brother. Not only my brother but also your brother. As was Ozil. You callously killed your own family for your personal gain. Now I feel only pity for you. God may find it in himself to forgive you. I don't believe I ever will."

Morana reacted with such malevolent anger and hatred that he took a few steps away from her. It was almost as if she was about to rise above the hole and consume him right there. She continued to thrash violently about, snarling and screaming like a beserker.

Suddenly her hand slipped from the crack in the rocky floor and she hung there with just her fingertips clinging to the side of the shaft. The sudden slip of her fingers caused her to immediately cease her violent gyrations and screaming.

Absolute silence descended upon the scene. Only the eerie light cast by the torch illuminated the macabre underground scene like a set from an old horror movie. Morana glared silently at Haaken, pure venomous hatred dripping like poison from her bloodshot eyes that were once so clear and beautiful.

Haaken spoke again, his voice as cold as ice. Colder than the winter wind blowing in from the north,

"Make your peace with the devil, Morana, he is expecting you soon..."

The torchlight faded as Haaken and Rocky made their way back to the mine entrance, leaving Morana staring blindly into the cold, silent darkness of her tomb.

Only the damp walls bore witness to her silent scream as she plunged to her violent death at the bottom of the shaft.

CHAPTER FORTY NINE

The Slaughtered Lamb.

Haaken and Rocky emerged from the darkness of the mine, into the cold fresh wind that brought winter ever closer to the mountains. Climbing into the Chevy with Rocky by his side, Haaken quietly lit another Cohiba then drove down to the twon of Goregate and Layla.

Layla heaved a huge sigh of relief to see Haaken and Rocky walk into the bar from the cold day outside. The icy blast of winter's frosty breath swirled past his muddy, denim clad legs and torn jacket. Quickly, he reached back to close the door, blotting out the bleak winter day and bent over to sweep the fine covering of early snow from Rocky's wet back.

Layla once again found her eyes trapped in his fierce, hypnotic gaze through hazel eyes that blazed with an intensity that now seemed to see only her. Her breath caught in her throat as he smiled at her. A tiny flash of gold glistened in the slightly tobacco-stained teeth. His bruised and scratched face held a slightly haunted look. To her, it was still a fine, ruggedly handsome face, framed by his snow speckled beard.

Layla stood nervously as Haaken purposefully strode across the room towards her, his eyes locked on hers. For the first time since they had met, Haaken bent to hug her tightly, then still holding her, stood up. Layla laughed, her feet dangling off the floor. Even Rocky wagged his stubby tail and large frame about in excitement.

Haaken gently placed Layla back on her feet and sat down on a bar stool with a slight grimace as his damaged ribs reminded him of the events leading up to this moment.

Haaken Hunter stared quietly into the mirror behind the bar for a moment. He felt as though he didn't know the tired, worn, and bruised face that stared back at him. A face with a haunted look of a man who had lost the joy of living a peaceful, mountain life.

Turning to Layla, who stood quietly watching him, Haaken spoke,

"It's time to go home…"

.

CHAPTER FIFTY

Three Months Later.

The cold front blowing in from the north had arrived with a wild flurry of snow and ice that now covered the landscape as far the eye could see. Much of the pine forest was now heavily burdened with snow, which had gathered and piled up on the branches.

A weak sun had broken through the thick cloud this morning to remind folks, that not too far off, summer would once again return and bring warmth to the land.

With Rocky sitting close by watching the forest, Haaken and Layla quietly stood in the mild sunlight near the three neatly arranged snow-covered graves not far up the slope behind the cabin.

Haaken had retrieved his Father's remains from the Double H Mine a few days after returning from Goregate. Harry Hunter now lay at peace next to Molly and Ulfred.

A cold, graveside funeral had been held in Goregate four days after Haaken had left town. The quiet funeral being held at Goregate cemetery went unnoticed as the town battened down for a cold winter. There were only three witnesses to Delilah's and Ozil's internment. The two grave diggers and the local Sheriff who had found her body after neighbours had reported a foul smell emanating from the house. As for Ozil, the Sheriff had been called out to retrieve his body from the Hunter homestead after he had apparently killed himself in an unfortunate accident while driving along one of the timber roads.

No one appeared to know the whereabouts of old Henry and Morana Renwick. They seemed to have simply vanished without a trace. The mangy old black cat still glared at the guests coming through the old revolving door of The Hotel Hope.

Haaken and Layla walked slowly, hand in hand, back down the slope to the cabin. Rocky was already trotting ahead of them, eager to curl up by the warm fireside.

Haaken Hunter paused for a moment on the porch while Layla and Rocky went inside ahead of him.

Standing there alone, he lit up a fine Cohiba Black Pequeños cigar and inhaled the ultra-smooth smoke, perfectly balanced and teeming with notes of cedar, sweet spice, and a splash of cafecíto. He looked out at the peaceful snow-covered forest as twin tendrils of smoke curled lazily from his nostrils. His hazel eyes reflected a moment of deep sadness before he turned to enter the warmth of the cabin.

The End.

Dear reader, I'm guessing if you are seeing this it means you have finished this book.

If so I really hope you enjoyed it!

Please do take a minute to leave a review on Amazon and Goodreads.

Your reviews really do help me to reach new readers as they are a form of social proof.

Feel free to come along and say hello on my Facebook page, which you can find by clicking here,

https://www.facebook.com/alexanderbutterfieldauthor

I love hearing from new readers! You will also hear of any new upcoming releases there.

Thank you very much once again, and rest assured, Haaken Hunter will return soon.

Printed in Great Britain
by Amazon